DAZZLING
THE AWARD-WINNING
ROMANCES OF
MARION CHESNEY

"All the elements for a good Regency come together....Witty, charming, touching."
—*Library Journal*

"Warm-hearted, hilarious reading."
—Baton Rouge *Sunday Magazine*

"Entertaining."
—*Booklist*

"Amusing."
—*Kirkus Reviews*

"Well-written and easy to read."
—*News-Sentinel*, Knoxville, TN

Also by Marion Chesney

Annabelle

Marion Chesney

ST. MARTIN'S PRESS/NEW YORK

Annabelle was previously published by Jove with the author pseudonym of Ann Fairfax.

ANNABELLE

ISBN: 0-312-91365-6   Can. ISBN: 0-312-91374-5

Printed in the United States of America

Jove edition/August 1980
First St. Martin's Press mass market edition/January 1989

10 9 8 7 6 5 4 3 2 1

For Harry Scott Gibbons
And Charles David Bravos Gibbons
With Love

Chapter One

MR. JAMES QUENNELL, the rector of Hazeldean, looked thoughtfully across the room at his eldest daughter, Annabelle, and wished for the hundredth time that he had not allowed himself to be coerced into sending the girl to London. This was to be Annabelle's last evening at home before her departure for the South in the morning.

If only they weren't so grindingly poor, if only he hadn't three other daughters to support, if only his good wife was not—well, why not admit it?—such a forceful and pushing woman.

And if only Annabelle were not so strikingly beautiful.

The soft light from the oil lamp in the shabby parlor of Hazeldean rectory cast a warm glow over Annabelle's features as she bent her head over her mending. She wore a simple round gown of cambric which had seen much wear, but even the shabby dress could not detract from the beauty of her voluptuous figure or take away an ounce of the startling effect of her creamy skin and masses of curly red-gold hair.

His other daughters, Mary, Susan, and Lisbeth, were all grouped around her. But they were as dark haired as their mother and had also inherited her sallow skin. The rector had timidly put forward the idea that one of the younger girls should go since Annabelle's beauty might prove to be more of a curse than a blessing, but his energetic wife had pooh-poohed the idea.

Mrs. Quennell had said in her usual strident manner, "The only thing we have in the bank is one beautiful daughter, and she should be used to the best advantage. Why send one of the others when you know they would not take?" This was all said with Mrs. Quennell's usual insensitivity to the feelings of her other, less-favored daughters.

The rector, as always, bowed to his wife's stronger will. Annabelle was to visit her godmother—a remote aristocratic connection on her mother's side of the family—and have a Season in London. She must catch a rich husband, or she would not be doing her duty as a Christian. Annabelle had meekly agreed to all plans for her future as she had meekly agreed to her mother's dictates from the day she was born. Even in the surrounding neighborhood, girls were married off every day to "suitable" gentlemen, and never once did the question of love or mutual esteem arise.

The only thing to raise doubts of any kind in Annabelle's eighteen-year-old mind was the fact that her mother shied away from any discussion about Annabelle's godmother—an unusual attitude in one so generally forthright. Godmother was Lady Emmeline, Dowager Marchioness of Eversley. What was she like? Mrs. Quennell had looked positively furtive. She couldn't remember. She had not seen the Dowager Marchioness in years.

Annabelle's last evening at home seemed like any other. Very few of her belongings had been packed since her godmother had written to say that a new wardrobe would be furnished.

And apart from the fact that her trunks were lying corded upstairs, no one would have guessed that one of the family was about to make a long and adventurous journey on the morrow.

Annabelle longed to have *someone—anyone—*to listen to her fears. What if she did not get married? What if her godmother should take her in dislike? But her sisters had banded together in their usual mutual envy of her beauty, and her mother had called her missish when she had tried to voice some of her doubts. Her father had merely pointed out that God would protect the innocent, leaving poor Annabelle to worry the more. Would He lean down from far above the clouds to protect a young girl during her first Season? Surely He had more important things to take care of than mere frivolities.

Annabelle looked round the shabby, cluttered parlor, at her three sisters tranquilly sure that life would be the same tomorrow as it was today, and her eyes misted with tears. The wind sighed in the old trees outside, and the grandfather clock in the corner seemed to tick away the seconds, faster and faster and faster, carrying her along on its racing heartbeats into the unknown tomorrow.

The Squire, Mr. Ralston, had kindly offered the use of his ancient and cumbersome travelling carriage and one of his wife's maids as chaperone.

That much, at least, was known. But what of the long miles to London? What of London itself? And what of her mysterious godmother?

Her detailed measurements and one of her old gowns had been posted to London months ago so that her wardrobe would be ready for her on her arrival. What her mother had written about her, Annabelle did not know, but in one of her letters of reply, the Dowager Marchioness had expressed her relief that the girl was "not an antidote."

The hollow chimes of the clock striking the hour roused Annabelle from her troubled thoughts. Her sisters were gathering up their sewing and yawning and stretching.

Mrs. Quennell indicated that it was time for bed but

signalled to Annabelle to remain after her sisters had gone upstairs.

She then fixed her daughter with her rather protruding stare. "This is the last chance I shall have to talk to you for some time, Annabelle," she began. "I must make sure that you understand the honor that is being done you. You *must*—it is *imperative* that you marry well. God has given you the advantage of beauty, and it must be put to use for the benefit of the family. You will obey your godmother *implicity* since she has assured me if you do exactly as she says, then you will be affianced by the end of the Season. I trust you have not filled your head with nonsense from romances and expect a young and handsome gentleman to fall in love with you. That is not the way of the world. Often girls of your age are comfortably married to men much older. Believe me, love fades when there is no money."

A look of pain passed over the gentle features of the rector. "And did your love fade?" he asked quietly, but his wife paid him not the smallest attention.

Annabelle shifted restlessly on her seat. She was used to lectures on her duty and young enough to look upon the task of marrying some man despite his age or manner as simply another kind of household chore. But she could not help wondering if her stern mother had ever felt any of the gentler passions. Often when her mother was lecturing her, Annabelle's mind slid away onto some more pleasant topic, seeing her mother silently forming the words as if on the other side of a thick pane of glass. As usual her brain blocked out the words of the lecture, but this time she studied Mrs. Quennell as if looking at a stranger.

A middle-aged woman with a trim figure, she wore her black hair tucked neatly away under a towering cap of starched muslin. Her pale weak eyes of washed-out blue must once have been as vivid a color as Annabelle's own before long evenings poring over the household accounts had faded them. Her mouth was thin and had a disappointed droop at the corners. She was not at all ill-favored for her years, but her rasping, bullying voice dominated all else. Annabelle looked over at her father and caught the look of hurt and distress on his features. He was essaying to speak—to find some loophole in the barrage of words.

"Father is trying to say something," interrupted Annabelle loudly in her clear, gentle voice. Never had anyone dared to interrupt Mrs. Quennell before, and she paused in amazement with her mouth open. The rector seized his opportunity.

"My dear," he said firmly, "let us make one thing quite clear. Annabelle is under no obligation to enter into any marriage contract distasteful to her. We shall contrive, come what may. There will always be a home here for her. I think we would be better employed in praying to God that our beloved daughter has a safe journey."

He bent his head in prayer, and his seething wife reluctantly followed his example. And while her husband's gentle words of prayer echoed round the parlor, Mrs. Quennell made an unchristian vow to herself that before her eldest daughter departed on her journey South, Miss Annabelle Quennell would be made to realise that no welcome *whatsoever* would be offered by her mother an' she should return unwed. As the rector voiced the "amen," Mrs. Quennell suddenly thought of the dangers of half-pay captains and other impoverished rattles in scarlet coats and would have reopened her lecture, but she opened her eyes to find that Annabelle had fled.

EARLY in the morning Annabelle slipped from the rectory with a long cloak wrapped round her. She wished to say good-bye to her home at a time of day when her mother's

5

angry voice and her sisters' envy were stilled with sleep.

The house looked large and graceful from the outside, more like the home of a country gentleman than what it was—a country rectory with small dark inconvenient rooms, bitterly cold in winter and stuffy and airless in summer. It was a low square building of mellow Georgian brick with a pillared entrance. The straggling, unkempt garden was shining under a white coating of freakish late spring frost, sparkling like rubies and diamonds under the red fire of the early morning sun. Smoke was beginning to rise lazily from the nearby village of Hazeldean which consisted of a row of houses on either side of an undragged byroad to York. The squat majesty of the Squire's Queen Anne mansion was at one end and the square Norman tower of her father's church was at the other.

Annabelle had a sudden wish to stay exactly where she was, frozen in place and time, neither going forwards nor backwards.

But London waited for her. London with its glittering Season, its mysterious godmother, and its possible suitor.

Annabelle was not much given to daydreaming, but she could not help hoping that perhaps she might meet some amiable gentleman on the road South from Yorkshire. That way she would not have to endure the terrors of a Season. He would be gentle and kind with a pleasant strong square face and *not* a terrifying aristocrat but one of the gentry like herself.

She was about to go in when her eye was arrested by what looked like an animated bundle of rags creeping along beside the hedge. She watched fascinated until the rags reared up and appeared to grow a head on top. It was Mad Meg from the gypsy encampment outside the town. She was feared and respected by the people of the village because of the uncanny accuracy of her predictions. But Annabelle knew that Meg's predictions came from assiduous news gathering rather than any supernatural psychic ability. She shrewdly guessed that Meg had heard of the proposed journey South and had come to go through the motions of reading her palm and telling her what she, Annabelle, and everyone else already knew. But Annabelle would no more have thought of spoiling Meg's act than she would of booing the village choir.

Meg came bustling up the weedy drive, her filthy features mercifully obliterated by the steam from her breath. She smelled overwhelmingly of woodsmoke, tar, cooked rabbit, and something else that a young lady such as Annabelle did not put a name to. "I have news for you, missie," cackled Meg, rolling her eyes wildly, every muscle on her face seen to be twitching as she got to very uncomfortable close quarters. Annabelle had once spied Meg in the middle of the gypsy encampment, happily dishing round the stew and behaving in a very normal manner. Her "madness" was all part of her routine.

"What is it, Meg. Tell me quickly!" said Annabelle, kindly feigning an excitement she did not feel and holding out her small work-roughened hand.

"What do I get?" asked Meg, suddenly stopping her twitching and eye rolling.

Annabelle felt in the pocket of her apron, and her fingers closed over a shilling. It *was* a lot of money to pay the old faker . . . but still . . . it was the last day. She held up the coin which Meg grabbed eagerly and stowed away somewhere in her rags. She bent her filthy head over Annabelle's hand.

"I see," she began to croon, "a long journey." She looked up suspiciously as something like a sigh came from Annabelle, but Annabelle stared back at her with a limpid expression.

"I see a long journey and at the end of it I see a rich world full of lords and dukes, and I see a handsome man waiting for you, missie." Again Meg glanced up. The gypsy was grateful for the shilling and suddenly felt an urge to do the job properly. She bent over the hand, concentrated on all the lore she had ever learned of palm reading, and was about to describe the tall, dark, and handsome suitor when something very strange happened.

The gypsy's grip on Annabelle's hand tightened painfully, and she raised her head again. But this time her eyes seemed to be turned inwards, horribly blind, and her old skin seemed to be stretched over her brittle bones to breaking point.

Her voice was high and thin, unlike her usual robust tones, and seemed to come from very, very far away. "There is terrible danger to your life from someone," moaned Meg, swaying back and forth. "First someone near to you . . . then you. Death by air, by fire, by water. All black death. But . . ."

"Annabelle!"

Mrs. Quennell's voice cut through the still frosty air. Annabelle pulled her hand away. She felt shaken and terribly cold.

"I must go, Meg," she whispered, glad to see the gypsy's eyes properly focused once more.

"Don't go. What happened? What did I say?" pleaded Meg wildly, but Annabelle was already off and running towards the house.

Chapter Two

BY THE TIME the Squire's coach had rumbled fifty miles on the road to the South, Annabelle had begun to relax. Her family seemed already a long way away, as if viewed mentally through the wrong end of a telescope. The Squire's maid, Bessie, had never been out of the village before and was happy and excited at the idea of a trip to "Lunnon." The carriage smelled rather strongly of hens, leading Annabelle to suspect it had recently done service as a temporary poultry coop, but it was comfortable for all that after one became used to the lurching, swaying motion.

Annabelle was still enough of a child to begin to view the visit to her godmother with some complacency. It would simply be a matter of obeying the Dowager Marchioness's instructions and then everything would be all right. She had been strictly taught to honor her father and mother, to obey her betters implicitly, and that no harm could come of doing one's duty. If she thought of Meg's prophecy at all, it was only to wonder what the old woman had been drinking.

But as mile followed weary mile and inexpensive posting house followed inexpensive posting house, Annabelle became increasingly nervous and tired of unaired beds and their attendant bugs. Even Bessie had at last fallen silent.

The weather grew warmer and the countryside increasingly flatter and greener and the turnpikes closer together.

A pale primrose twilight was bathing the grimy streets with gold as the heavy creaking coach rumbled its way down into the north of London. With eyes gritty with fatigue Annabelle tried to focus on the strange and noisy sights until her eyelids began to droop. The carriage was momentarily halted in traffic; a pieman with a loaded tray bobbed past the window of the coach, the pies steaming in the chill evening air. Then Annabelle fell asleep to wake an hour later and realise that they had finally come to a stop and the journey was at an end.

She climbed stiffly down from the coach and stood on the pavement with trembling legs. Flambeaux placed in brackets on the wall blazed outside an imposing mansion with a glossy white-painted door with a shining brass knocker. The whole house was ablaze with lights, and turning round, Annabelle could see the blackness of the gardens of Berkeley Square.

The door was opened after an energetic rat-tat on the knocker by the Squire's groom to reveal the tall, imposing figure of a bewigged butler. He eyed Annabelle's shabby bonnet and worn pelisse and raised his eyebrows. Butlers, Annabelle was to learn, hardly ever trouble themselves to ask unnecessary questions. They simply raise their eyebrows, the level denoting the importance of the question.

This butler's eyebrows ran up his corrugated forehead and disappeared under his powdered wig. Annabelle found she could not manage to say a word. But the Yorkshire groom was not going to be put down by an uppity London servant.

"Doan't stand there gawking, man," he said tersely. "This here is Miss Quennell."

The eyebrows dropped. The butler inclined his head

a bare millimeter to indicate that miss was to enter. With a slightly deepening incline he indicated that she was to wait.

"Oh, miss," breathed Bessie. "Ain't it *grand*."

The hallway did seem imposing even to the tired Annabelle. Beeswax candles blazed from sconces in the walls and were reflected in the black and white tiles of the floor. A beautiful marble staircase covered in a thick turkey red carpet rose gracefully to the upper floors. A huge fire crackled briskly on the hearth.

The double doors leading to a room on the left swung open, and the butler appeared again. Again he did not speak but merely stood to one side of the open doors. With her heart in her mouth Annabelle walked forward into the room.

The room was as graceful as the hall with pale green walls, elegant Chippendale furniture, a marble Adam fireplace, and various Eversley ancestors staring down in high-nosed disdain from their gilt frames. But Annabelle only had eyes for the extraordinary figure who was coming to meet her. This could surely not be the Dowager Marchioness of Eversley! She had curls of a wildly improbable shade of gold peeping out from beneath a frivolous lace cap, and her heavy square face was rouged and painted like a mask. She was dressed in a pale pink Indian muslin dress cut very low to expose an acreage of bony bosom and—oh, horrors—she had *damped* her dress to reveal all the whalebone charms of a tight French corset and the billows of flesh above and below it.

Annabelle looked wildly round, hoping some other, more soberly dressed lady might emerge, but a high girlish giggle emerged from this lady's painted mouth and she simpered awfully, "I declare, Annabelle Quennell, you do not believe I could be your godmother. You must not mind, my dear. I am accustomed to people finding me 'strordinarily *young*. Come and kiss me."

Annabelle nervously complied, noticing as she drew back that her lips had left a barren patch in the mask of powder.

The Dowager Marchioness stretched up her gloved arms and removed Annabell's hat and then stood back and stared in satisfaction at the wealth of red-gold hair.

"Beautiful," she murmured. "Just as your mama promised. Well, that's settled. 'Course, had you been *plain*, I should have had the terrible bore of posting you back to Yorkshire. Now, off with you and change. We will be late for the opera."

Annabelle looked at her faintly and then at the little gilt clock on the mantelshelf. "B-but, I had hoped to retire, Godmother. Perhaps a tray in my room . . ."

"Nonsense! I have the finest beau in all London waiting to meet you. Ha! That makes you stare. Yes, I have picked out a suitor for you, and you shall meet him this very evening! Now, do as you are told, child." She touched a bell on the wall. "Your rooms are ready, and you will find my lady's maid, Horley, waiting to help you with your dress. Your beau's name is Captain Jimmy MacDonald of the Eighteenth Hussars. I know he can hardly wait to meet you!"

"I CAN hardly wait to meet her," drawled Captain Jimmy MacDonald from the depths of his chair.

"One would think you were uninterested in meeting anything other than another bottle of claret," replied the light, amused voice of Lord Sylvester Varleigh. "Who is she?"

The Captain looked gloomily round the Great Subscription Room of Brooks's in St. James's. "Oh, Emmeline's dragging some filly to the opera tonight," he yawned. "Wants me to marry her."

"She must be very rich," murmured Lord Varleigh, looking down at the sprawling figure of the Captain. The Captain's pockets were always notoriously to let.

"Ain't got a penny," said the Captain, "but I promised to oblige." Lord Varleigh raised his thin eyebrows in surprise but was forestalled from further comment by the Captain adding wrathfully, "And stop hovering over me like some great demned horrible bird of prey."

There was indeed something rather hawklike about the Lord's thin white face with its hooded lids and high-bridged nose. By contrast the Captain's tanned and handsome face, under a mop of carefully curled hair gleaming with Macassar oil, was bordered by luxurious side-whiskers and made him look exactly what he was—a soldier in peacetime who loathed every minute of it. With the cessation of hostilities with France, he had launched himself on the London social scene with all the enthusiasm he had applied to a Peninsular campaign and had subsequently found it stale, flat, and infinitely unprofitable.

His face flushed with the amount of claret he had consumed, the Captain looked round the famous club with a jaundiced eye. Apart from four painted panels by Antonio Zucchi, the walls were bare. "Why don't they brighten up this mausoleum with some pictures?" he said irritably.

"Because," said Lord Varleigh soothingly, "pictures would distract the gamblers."

"Oh, well," grumped the Captain, refilling his glass, "what else can one expect from a club founded by a lot of demned Macaronis?"

The Macaronis were the dandies of the last century,

so called because they had made the Grand Tour which had included a visit to Italy. "All they did," pursued the Captain, "was to bring back a dish that looks like a pile of demned great white worms."

"They also invented the slang word 'bore,' " pointed out Lord Varleigh, much amused.

"Meaning I'm one," retorted the Captain good-naturedly. "Well, I'd better get going or I'll never hear the end of it from Emmeline. Don't even know this gel's background. She's probably as common as a barber's chair."

He half rose from his seat only to be pushed down into it again by a fellow officer, Major Timothy Wilks. "You still as good with your fives?" roared the Major. "Feel like a bout at Jackson's tomorrow?"

"Wallop you any time you feel like it, dear boy," said the Captain, the prospect of a boxing match causing him to show enthusiasm for the first time that evening. "Only fair to tell you, though. Was trained by Mendoza."

"Pooh! That Israelite cannot top Jackson."

"Mendoza is infinitely superior in regards to dexterity," said the Captain wrathfully.

"He has a remarkably quick eye. He strikes oftener and stops better than any man in England . . ."

"He's weak in the loins," rejoined the Major.

"But he is finely formed in the breast and arms," said the Captain enthusiastically. "Why, I remember . . ."

"Your meeting at Covent Garden," interrupted Lord Varleigh with a gentle reminder.

"Oh, stuff," said Captain MacDonald. "Look—I'll be a trifle late. You're going anyway, ain't you, Varleigh? Present my compliments and say I'll be along directly. Oh, and if the gel's Friday-faced, send a messenger to warn me."

"Very well," smiled Lord Varleigh, thinking, not for

the first time, what an overgrown schoolboy the Captain was. "I shall tell her you can hardly wait to meet her!"

ANNABELLE looked at her reflection in the long pier glass and turned to Horley in dismay.

"I cannot wear this gown," she said firmly. "It is . . . it's *indecent*."

The evening gown was admittedly of the finest silk velvet in a delectable shade of pale green and opened down the front to reveal an underdress of gold silk. The neckline, though bordered with a creamy fall of old lace, was more of a waistline! thought Annabelle bitterly. It seemed to leave not only her shoulders but most of her bosom bare.

Annabelle had revived somewhat from the fatigues of her journey at the sight of the splendor of her new quarters. She was to be the proud possessor of a sitting room and a large bedroom with an old-fashioned powder room beyond. Thick oriental rugs covered the floor, and pretty flock wallpaper adorned the walls. Fires burned in both bedroom and sitting room, adding their light to the blaze of beeswax candles on the walls. Her hair had been expertly and becomingly dressed by her godmother's lady's maid, Horley, and the dress, spread out innocently over a high-backed chair, had seemed beautiful.

"There is nothing up with it," said Horley severely. "To think of all the trouble and expense your godmama's gone to—why, she will think you downright ungrateful!"

Annabelle felt obscurely that the woman was being impertinent but did not have the courage to protest any longer.

The Dowager Marchioness, Lady Emmeline, surveyed her goddaughter with pleasure. Those wide innocent blue eyes, combined with the daring sophistication of the dress, were alluring in the extreme, decided the old lady with satisfaction. No, Annabelle may not have a shawl. The lightest of gauze wraps was all that was necessary.

THE famous opera house was crowded. No one seemed to be paying much attention to the performance on stage as they whispered and shuffled and hopped from box to box. Lady Emmeline stared round the dimness of the house. "Can't see the rascal," she whispered to Annabelle. "But he'll come . . . never fear."

That's just what I *am* afraid of, thought poor Annabelle. She dreaded the interval when the lights would be lit. Her entrance to the opera house had been enough. Every male eye had seemed to fasten on her bosom and shoulders, and everyone quite blatantly discussed her.

"That must be him," said Lady Emmeline, hearing a sound at the back of the box. She twisted round. "Oh, it's *you*, Varleigh. Where's MacDonald?"

"He will be here directly," said a light, amused voice. "He assured me he could hardly wait to meet Miss . . ."

"Miss Quennell," snapped Lady Emmeline, ungraciously making the introductions. Annabelle quickly looked up into Lord Varleigh's light gray eyes and then dropped her own in confusion. What a terrifying man!

Lady Emmeline was still attired in the damped pink muslin, but Annabelle's sharp eyes had already noticed several other ladies just as daringly attired. Certainly they were younger and mostly in the lower boxes. She became aware that Lord Varleigh was speaking to her. "Miss Quennell," came the light, pleasant voice from somewhere behind her, "when did you arrive in London?"

"This evening," said Annabelle without turning her head.

"And where did you journey from?" pursued the voice.

"From Yorkshire, my lord."

"Yorkshire! You must indeed be fatigued. But then, I gather you are anxious to meet Captain MacDonald."

Annabelle was about to reply a dutiful "yes," but the beginnings of a very tiny spark of rebellion stopped her.

"I do not know Captain MacDonald," she said coldly. "He is a friend of my godmother."

"Indeed!" mocked the voice as the house lights were lit for the interval. "Then you are in for a pleasant surprise. Here comes the Captain."

Annabelle stared round the house and became aware of a terrific commotion in the boxes opposite. A young man in evening dress had jumped onto the ledge of a box and with unerring agility was making his way towards her by walking nimbly along the edges of the boxes. With a final leap he made the parapet of Annabelle's box and stood looking down at her in open, if somewhat drunken, admiration. Annabelle felt herself engulfed by the blush of all time as the Captain climbed into the box and pulled up a chair beside her.

Then she became aware that several high-nosed ladies were staring at the Captain in open admiration. Annabelle shook her head slightly in amazement. It was her first lesson in the strange double standards of London society. The noisier and more vulgar the display, the more the man was considered no end of a young blood. Boorishness betokened masculinity and *joie de vivre*. But pity help any *woman* who dared to follow suit. She would be labelled "a sad romp," a country bumpkin, no better than a washerwoman.

I must be too nice in my ideas—too countrified, thought poor Annabelle.

"Off with you, Varleigh," the Captain was saying.

"As you can see, I am well suited."

Lady Emmeline had noticed the Captain's admiration and Annabelle's blush and was purring with contentment. "My lord," she said, holding up a small plump hand. "We are having supper afterwards to welcome Annabelle to London. Please join us."

Lord Varleigh hesitated. The warm charms of his mistress, Lady Jane Cherle, beckoned. But he was intrigued by this milk and water miss in the daring gown and murmured his acceptance. He bent punctiliously over Annabelle's hand and allowed his hard gray eyes to stray insolently over her neck and bosom. Annabelle drew her gauze shawl tightly round her shoulders and stared back at him, her large eyes wide with shame. Lord Varleigh had a sudden feeling that he was behaving badly but after all, what else did the girl expect, dressed as she was?

The rest of the opera passed like a nightmare. The Captain had drawn his chair so close to Annabelle that his thigh was uncomfortably pressed against her own. She moved her chair several times, but each time the Captain pursued by moving his own chair.

Worse was to come when they returned to Lady Emmeline's house in Berkeley Square. The only sober member of the party of gentlemen appeared to be Lord Varleigh. The Captain, his friend the Major, and a vacuous young gentleman rejoicing in the name of George Louch were definitely *bowzy*, thought Annabelle as she sat in her aunt's drawing room, trembling with cold and fatigue. A cheerful fire was blazing up the chimney, but Annabelle had retreated to the chilly corner of the room in the hope of escaping attention.

With a sinking feeling she saw Lord Varleigh coming towards her. In the full blaze of candlelight she saw him to be a very tall man in faultless evening clothes who wore his thick fair hair unpowdered but in a longer style than the current fashion. He had a singular charm of manner of which he was aware. He turned the full impact of it on the bewildered Annabelle, extracting information on her home and family with expert ease. But to his surprise he noticed for once that his charm was not having its usual effect. The lady was staring into space, and it was with no little feeling of pique that he realised she was trying to stifle a yawn. He had an impulse to tease her, to rouse the sleeping beauty from her gently bred apathy.

He waved his quizzing glass towards the group at the fireplace who were surrounding the grotesquely giggling and coquetting Lady Emmeline. "It seems as if your Captain is about to favor us with a tune."

Annabelle opened her mouth to protest that the gentleman was not *her* Captain, but Jimmy MacDonald had launched into song.

Holding onto the mantel and seemingly oblivious of the roaring fire scorching his knee breeches, he began to sing in a loud, penetrating bass voice:

> Here's a health to our Monarch and long may he reign,
> The blessing of England, its boast and its pride;
> May his Troops grace the land, and his Fleets rule the
>   main,
> And may Charlotte long sit on the throne at his side.

This was received with cheers and much clinking of glasses.

Much flushed with wine and with his powdered hair almost standing on end, Mr. George Louch protested, "I prefer the songs of *wit* rather than patriotism." In a surprisingly soprano voice he began to sing:

> 'Tis said that our soldiers so lazy are grown,
> With luxury, plenty and ease,

That they more for their carriage than courage are known.
And they scarce know the use of a *piece*.

Let them say what they will, since it nobody galls,
And exclaim still louder and louder,
But there ne'er was more money expended in *balls*,
Or a greater consumption of *powder*.

"I resent that," said the Captain fiercely. "How dare you mock the soldiers of England, sirrah!" He staggered forward and raised his gloves to strike the startled Mr. Louch on the cheek; then he swayed ludicrously for a few moments, and obviously forgetting what he was about to do, collapsed into an armchair and fell sound asleep.

"What a man!" sighed Lady Emmeline. "Ah, if I were only a few years younger . . . You are a lucky girl, Annabelle."

Lord Varleigh watched Annabelle's expressive face. The proposed match obviously was not to her taste. So what was behind it all? The Captain had no money and neither had Miss Quennell. They were obviously not in love. Somehow, he decided, Lady Emmeline must be pulling the strings of her handsome puppets. It might prove to be a marionette show worth watching. The Major and Mr. Louch were hauling the drunken Captain to his feet.

"I am sure you shall be all the rage, Annabelle," went on Lady Emmeline. "We may even ask Mr. Brummell to dine."

"Who is Mr. Brummell?" asked Annabelle, moving from her corner towards the fireplace.

"Why, you innocent," laughed Lady Emmeline. "Mr. Brummell is the Leader of Fashion. It is to be hoped he will not give you one of his famous setdowns. If only he would come here. It is said he rarely dines at home."

Annabelle felt tired and cold, and humiliated by the indecency of her gown. "Indeed!" she said sweetly. "Then it could be said that Mr. Brummell never opens his mouth except at the expense of another."

Lord Varleigh put his hand to his mouth to hide a smile. So the milk and water miss had a tongue after all. He bowed gracefully and begged for permission to call.

"I suppose so," said Lady Emmeline ungraciously. "But she's spoken for—mind."

After the gentlemen had left, Annabelle remembered to ask about the welfare of the Squire's maid, Bessie.

"She is very well, I trust," said Lady Emmeline with a sudden cavernous yawn. "She will, of course, return to Yorkshire as soon as the horses are rested. Do not trouble your pretty head over the affairs of rustic domestics, my dear. Tell me. Are you not pleased with the Captain? Is he not a fine and dashing man?"

"Yes, indeed," faltered Annabelle. "I did promise my parents I would try to make an *advantageous* marriage."

"Well, and so you shall," snapped Lady Emmeline. "You will get my money if you marry the Captain as lord knows he has none of his own. If you do not—then you may find your way back to Yorkshire."

She saw the alarm on the girl's face and felt she had gone too far too soon. "I shall not press you, Annabelle," added Lady Emmeline. "You shall have your Season and enjoy all the balls and parties. But you see, the Captain's father was a great friend of mine, and I feel it my duty to keep an eye on his son. Jimmy MacDonald is undoubtably too wild, but he will soon settle down."

"His manner is somewhat frightening," said Annabelle, trying to choose her words carefully. "Lord Varleigh seems more, perhaps, the gentleman."

"Varleigh!" sneered the Dowager Marchioness. "A bloodless aristocrat. I like a man with a bit of fire. The only thing to say in Varleigh's favor is that he keeps Lady Jane Cherle as mistress, and he must have some stamina to mount that one."

Annabelle felt suddenly immeasurably tired and sad.

Chapter Three

ANNABELLE WAS NOT to see either Lord Varleigh or Captain Jimmy MacDonald for the next two days. She had contracted a feverish cold and was obliged to keep to her bedchamber.

The Captain sent a whole hothouse of flowers to the invalid, but the effect of his generosity was somewhat marred by Lady Emmeline muttering under her breath about being dunned by the florist. Much more welcome was a present of Miss Jane Austen's *Pride and Prejudice* from Lord Varleigh. Annabelle had never read a novel in her life before, despite her mother's conviction that she had somehow managed to obtain the forbidden volumes on the quiet. She turned to the opening page and plunged in headfirst. The sights and sounds of the square outside faded before the interesting present and magic of Elizabeth Bennet and the supercilious Mr. Darcy.

After two days, when her fever abated, she was allowed to transfer herself downstairs to a daybed by the window in the drawing room, where she could view the comings and goings of fashionable society in the square. She had finished the novel the previous day and passed the time by studying the passersby for that young man with the square tanned face who would rescue her from the prospect of marriage to the Captain.

But the bucks and bloods who promenaded the square were startling and frightening creatures to the country-bred Annabelle.

A young man of high society, if he were on his own, seemed to walk around the square with as much consequence as if the houses he passed all belonged to him. The idea also seemed to be to turn into Berkeley Square in such a hurry that the buck would have a chance of dashing himself against some well-dressed woman or elderly gentleman and hurling them into the filth of the kennel in the road. If raining, the sport seemed to be to dip your cane into a puddle and flick it under your arm so that if you did not blind the person behind you, you might at least have the satisfaction of flicking muddy water all over his clothes.

The most distressing thing they seemed to find to do, these swells of society and Pinks of the *ton*, was to make water in the most public place possible, especially if a party of young ladies happened to be passing.

Annabelle had mentioned her shock and dismay at the latter spectacle to her godmother, but Lady Emmeline had only given her terrible girlish laugh and pointed out that ladies could not be offended when they see—*nothing*. A well-bred gentlewoman was not, of course, aware of this necessary human function, so naturally nothing at all could have taken place.

All too soon her short period of convalescence was over. The Season had begun. Almack's opening Wednesday was not due for another week. The Egremonts' ball in Grosvenor Square was that evening, a sparkling social event. The Captain would be calling to escort Annabelle. The notice of her engagement had been posted in the *Gazette* so it would be quite the form for her to perform the waltz with her fiancé, said Lady Emmeline.

Annabelle rose trembling to her feet and held up her hand to stop this flow of news and instruction as Lady Emmeline happily rattled on. "I have not been properly consulted on the matter of my engagement, ma'am," she said in a trembling voice. "I have not had a chance to become acquainted with Captain MacDonald and so far, what I have seen has not endeared him to me. I have not had time to consult my father on the matter, nor my feelings."

"Pooh, fiddlesticks!" said Lady Emmeline, little knowing how much this small assertive effort had cost her young guest. "Don't fret about it," laughed Lady Emmeline, "you'll come about. You'll discover you are the envy of every girl in London. Mark my words!"

"But to announce my betrothal in such a hurly-burly fashion . . . ," began Annabelle.

Lady Emmeline surveyed the flushed and angry girl, and her eyes narrowed. "I should have thought that a girl reared in a rectory would have a better sense of duty," she said. "I have gone to considerable expense to furnish you with an attractive wardrobe and to affiance you to one of the most dashing men in London, and you repay me by *sulking* like the veriest child!"

"Indeed, I am t-truly s-sorry, Godmother," stammered Annabelle, near to tears. She was still too young to realise that doing one's duty did not necessarily mean obeying every single dictate made by a more senior adult.

"There, there, we will say no more about it. Now I note you are wearing one of your old gowns. This will not do *at all*. I told Madame Croke to supply me with the *dashingest* wardrobe for you, and although I have not examined it myself, I am sure it would be a vast improvement on what you are wearing."

Annabelle meekly said, "Yes, Godmother," while her mind worked furiously. If her godmother had not seen the wardrobe, then it might be possible to make some discreet alterations. Annabelle was an excellent needle-woman.

"Oh, and while I remember," went on Lady Emme-

25

line, 'it would be better if you called me 'Emmeline.' 'Godmother' is *so* aging. We are almost the same age after all." And with that stunning remark Lady Emmeline took herself from the room.

DESPITE Annabelle's fears the Captain did not seem to think it necessary to call on her during the day. She found an opportunity to ask Horley early in the afternoon which of her gowns she would be wearing to the Egremonts' ball. The dress, when produced, looked deceptively simple. Of heavy white satin, it was high-waisted in the current mode and trimmed with tiny seed pearls and gold thread. Annabelle dismissed Horley and tried it on as soon as the lady's maid's footsteps had faded down the corridor. As she had suspected, the bosom was again too low, the combination of virginal white and sophisticated cut making her appear shockingly *fast*. Madame Croke, the dressmaker, must indeed be a kind of depraved genius, thought Annabelle grimly, little realising that that was probably the first hard and uncharitable thought about anyone that had ever entered her young brain.

She pulled open the drawers, looking for some material. Her new undergarments frothed and foamed with white lace. Annabelle surveyed them for a few minutes and then carefully began to unpick some exquisite white lace from the leg of a pair of drawers. Then sitting beside the window to catch the best light, she began to stitch the lace into the bosom of her ball gown with nimble and expert fingers.

When Annabelle entered the drawing room that night, Lady Emmeline was fortunately too excited to notice that her young guest's ball gown was strangely demure in style for one of Madame Croke's creations.

"Only look, my dear," she cried, holding out a piece

of paper. "It is prodigious exciting. I have an unknown admirer."

The paper contained a few short unsigned lines.

> Please accept these flowers,
> They come from one who loves you,
> Be seated in Diana's bower,
> Until he comes.

"'Diana's bower,'" read Annabelle. "It doesn't make much sense."

"Oh, but it does," giggled Lady Emmeline. "There is to be a classical theme in the decoration of the Egremonts' ball. Gods and goddesses, you know. Ah! Diana—chaste and fair." She pirouetted round the room in a girlish debutante dress of filmy white muslin embroidered with rosebuds which revealed all the charms of a black corset and little else underneath.

"And look at the flowers—lilies, I declare."

Annabelle felt horribly embarrassed. Someone must be playing an unkind joke. But then she did not yet know London society. Perhaps elderly matrons with brassy curls were all the crack.

Captain MacDonald was announced, and Lady Emmeline delivered herself of a lame excuse and left them alone. The Captain was looking very handsome in black and white evening dress with a fine diamond pin winking at his stock. The pin was an engagement present from Lady Emmeline which she had given him with the curt reminder that it would be in the worst taste to take it immediately to the pawnbroker.

He nervously twisted his side-whiskers round one broad finger and eyed the girl in front of him with some trepidation.

"Well, here we are—all engaged, right and tight."

"It has all been too sudden," said Annabelle, equally nervous. "I hardly know you."

"Oh, we'll be seeing lots of each other before we tie the knot," said the Captain blithely. "Fell in love with you at first sight, 'pon my soul I did."

"Lady Emmeline has *commanded* me to marry you," said Annabelle in a low voice.

"Put that way, it sounds a bit dismal," said the Captain, espying a decanter of Madeira in the corner and feeling that life had taken a rosier turn. Should he kiss her before he had a drink? Better. Some females didn't like the smell of the stuff.

He advanced and grasped her firmly round the waist and planted a warm kiss on her mouth. It was like kissing a statue. Well, the money that Emmeline would leave her would pay for many a pretty ladybird.

But the girl seemed to have turned very white and faint. Perhaps she had been moved by his kiss after all.

The Captain poured out two glasses of Madeira with an expert hand and carried one to Annabelle. She stiffly took the glass like a marionette and drained the contents.

"That's the stuff," said Captain MacDonald enthusiastically. "Ain't been kissed before?"

Annabelle shook her head dumbly.

"You'll soon get used to it, heh! You'll find me accounted a ladies man. Even the Prince Regent himself will tell you. "Pon rep, Jimmy MacDonald is a terror with the ladies."

Annabelle smiled faintly. "Terror" was indeed the right word. But perhaps it was merely because of her inexperience. The wine had given her false courage, and she tried to assure herself she would get used to the Captain in time.

"You'll like being married, you'll see," said the large Captain, pacing up and down the room with his replenished glass in his hand. "We'll buy a neat little house right in Town and we can do a bit of entertaining. Got to ask the Colonel and his wife, of course, before anybody else." He paused and looked at Annabelle. She really was remarkably beautiful with that incredible hair and voluptuous figure. He realised he had let his eyes roam too freely and turned his attention to his glass.

"You musn't mind Emmeline pushing you around," he said in a kindly voice. "Fact is—the old girl's fond of me. The old Marquess, Emmeline's husband, was a famous soldier, you know, and Emmeline favors the military. Known her since I was so high. She bought me my first pair of colors. Don't know what I would do without her and that's a fact," he added gruffly.

Annabelle found herself warming to him. "I am also very grateful to Godmother," she said quietly. "She has really gone to a great deal of effort on my behalf."

"Wouldn't have done if you'd been an antidote," said the Captain. "Only the best would do for old Jimmy."

At that moment the Dowager Marchioness came tit-tupping in, clutching her bouquet and eager to tell her new audience about her unknown admirer. "Lilies, eh!" said the Captain. "Funny sort of flower to send. Must have thought it was your funeral. Joke, that's all," he added hurriedly as Emmeline gave him a steely look. "Shall we go?"

THE Egremonts' ballroom was indeed decorated in the classical manner. Captain MacDonald gallantly scrawled his name several times in Annabelle's dance card before escaping to the card room. Lady Emmeline headed straight for Diana's bower which was in a secluded corner of the ballroom. A pretty arbor with a small sofa, it was partly concealed from the rest of the ballroom by masses of flowers. Behind the sofa a marble statue of Diana, goddess of the chase, stood complete with marble bow and marble hounds.

29

Annabelle had little time to take in the splendor of the ballroom with its glittering and elegant guests, its French chalked floor and great banks of hothouse flowers. Soon she was surrounded by admirers, and by the time the orchestra struck up, her dance card was full.

How handsome and courteous the gentlemen seemed! Not at all like the bucks and bloods she had watched promenading in the square. There was admittedly quite a sprinkling of fops with their extraordinary wigs, stiff-skirted coats, and high red heels mincing and tittupping around the edges of the floor. The famous Mr. Brummell was pointed out to her by one partner, and Annabelle thought he looked surprisingly amusing and amused, and not at all like the terrifying Leader of Fashion she had been led to expect.

She dipped and turned, curtseyed in the dance, moving increasingly easier as she became accustomed to partnering a gentleman and not one of her sisters on the sanded parlor floor of the rectory. The only thing that made her feel uncomfortable was the fact that several of the ladies kept staring at her gown and then putting their bejewelled and feathered heads together. Then she noticed Lord Varleigh standing at the entrance of the ballroom. His evening dress looked as if it had been molded to his tall muscular form, and his light gray eyes raked over the dancers searching for someone. Annabelle, perhaps!

She felt quite breathless when the dance ended but put it down to the energetic steps of the Scottish reel she had just performed. He was coming towards her. He stopped and gave her a singularly sweet smile accompanied by a bow. Then he moved on.

"You are looking more enchanting than ever, my dear," Annabelle heard him say in a caressing voice. But the words were not said to her. Lord Varleigh had come to a stop beside a ravishing brunette. Her pink satin gown clung to her shapely figure, and her low neckline revealed magnificent breasts. Annabelle glanced down at her own lace-covered bosom and wondered if she had been too missish. The dashing brunette was a shade on the plump side. Probably be as fat as a sow by the time she's forty, thought Annabelle and then wondered why she should so vehemently dislike a lady she did not even know. The brunette was dimpling up at Lord Varleigh in the most enchanting way from under thick black eyelashes.

Annabelle became aware that she was staring at the couple quite blatantly. She blushed and turned away to look for her next partner.

The gallant Captain came bounding up exuding a strong smell of the best Burgundy and Rowlandson's Macassar Oil.

"It is the waltz," said Annabelle, listening to the announcement. "I fear I do not know how to do it."

"It's easy," said Captain MacDonald, putting an arm round her waist. "I lead . . . you follow."

Once Annabelle had become accustomed to the strange feeling of a man's arm round her waist, she began to enjoy her first waltz. There was no denying that the Captain's agility at Covent Garden extended to the ballroom, and Annabelle floated happily in his arms, executing turns and twists she would have believed impossible some few minutes before. As she relaxed, Annabelle suddenly thought of Emmeline. She had not seen the Dowager Marchioness for some time.

"Have you seen my godmother?" she asked the Captain, looking up anxiously into his eyes.

"Oh, *she'll* be all right," he said carelessly, drawing Annabelle closer in his arms. "I say, let's speed things up a bit. This dance is dashed slow!"

He began to spin faster and faster until Annabelle could not tell which way she was going. She finally managed to focus her eyes and notice that they were spinning rapidly towards a bower dedicated to Venus rising from the sea. A statue of the goddess on her shell stood in the middle of a small pool of water.

"Stop!" cried Annabelle frantically. The Captain paid no heed. He was tum-tumming the music of the waltz so loudly that he could not hear anything other than the sound of his own voice.

Annabelle wrenched herself free just in time. There was a tremendous splash as Captain MacDonald tripped over the flower-bedecked edge of the pool and tumbled headlong in.

The dancers stopped dancing and clustered round, laughing and cheering. The Captain heaved himself to his feet and pretended to wash himself while the admiring crowd urged him to further efforts. Annabelle wished fiercely the silly clown would disappear. She was pink with embarrassment. It was worse than being affianced to Grimaldi.

With a final bow and flourish Captain Jimmy MacDonald climbed out of the pool to go and change. The interrupted waltz started up again. Annabelle heard a quiet amused voice in her ear. "Shall I partner you for the finish of the dance, Miss Quennell?" Lord Varleigh was looking down at her, his eyes alight with mockery.

She drew back. "No, my lord, I am now convinced I cannot waltz."

"Then I shall unconvince you," he said, taking her firmly in his arms. "I am less energetic than Jimmy, but you will find my quieter steps easier to follow."

What a peculiar world, thought Annabelle, where gentlemen could not seem to take a simple "no" for an answer. But Lord Varleigh was remarkably easy to follow, although she felt almost painfully conscious of the pressure of his gloved hand at her waist.

"And what do you think of your first London ball, Miss Quennell?" Lord Varleigh asked the red-gold head bent beneath his. She raised her head, and he was again startled by her beauty. "If I were a less experienced man," he thought, "my heart might be in some danger!" He suddenly realised that she was not giving the conventional return to his greeting.

"It's their eyes," Annabelle was saying, and he wondered what she had said before. "I suppose that is what distinguishes the *ton* from the ordinary people. They have such hard, insolent eyes. Who is that vastly pretty lady over there?"

Lord Varleigh followed her gaze. "Lady Jane Cherle," he said shortly. Annabelle looked at the dashing brunette she had noticed earlier in the evening, blushed and said "oh" in a small voice.

He swore under his breath. So Lady Emmeline had been gossiping, had she? Well, what did it matter? Jane was no milk and water miss. She was all fire and passion. She . . . He looked fondly over to where his mistress was standing, surrounded by her customary court of gallants, and frowned. She was surely older than he had thought.

"I did not know she was your particular . . . er . . . friend," Annabelle was saying. "Or I should not have asked."

"All the world knows Lady Jane is my . . . er . . . particular friend," he said lightly. "That is a vastly becoming gown."

Now what had he said to make the girl blush. He had only spoken the truth. The foaming white inset of lace at her bosom was vastly alluring in a very feminine way, a great improvement on the scandalous gown she had worn to the opera.

His eyes strayed again to where Lady Jane was standing, and Annabelle had a sudden feeling of pique. She sought for some way to regain his attention.

"I have seen Mr. Brummell," she ventured, "and he seems a very unassuming young man."

"Appearances can be very deceptive," murmured Lord Varleigh, executing a neat turn. "Take yourself, for example, Miss Quennell. Can it be that you are not the shy, sedate country miss you appear?"

His eyes again strayed in the direction of his mistress.

"And can it be that my Lord Varleigh is not the libertine he would appear to be?" countered Annabelle sweetly.

He looked down at her with his pale eyes narrowed. "Do not confuse impertinence with wit, Miss Quennell. I can think of nothing more boring."

"Then perhaps you would rather dance with some other lady," snapped Annabelle.

"Perhaps," he rejoined lazily. "But then, I am a poor slave to the conventions, and it would not do your social consequence any good if I walked from the floor and left you standing."

"Are you then so socially powerful?" demanded Annabelle.

"Yes," he replied with infuriating simplicity. And then, "I do wish the Egremonts had thought to employ the services of a chimney sweep before embarking on this ball. There is a dreadful smell of smoke. Why, it is like a . . ."

But whatever else Lord Varleigh was about to say was drowned by a piercing scream.

Black smoke began to swirl across the ballroom. Several hysterical voices shouted, "Fire!" and Lady Jane Cherle in the neatest way possible staggered across the short distance that separated her from Lord Varleigh and fainted into his arms.

Then Annabelle heard cries of "Lady Emmeline! It's Lady Emmeline!"

She plunged in the direction of the smoke which was pouring from Diana's bower. A figure, dimly recognisable as Lady Emmeline, was being rolled across the floor by two young officers trying to extinguish the flames on her dress. Footmen were hurrying forward with wooden pails of water and throwing them on the still blazing silk hangings which hung behind the now soot-begrimed marble statue of Diana.

Unmindful of her ballgown, Annabelle knelt beside the grotesque figure of the Dowager Marchioness. "Oh, what happened?" she whispered. Lady Emmeline slowly opened one eye and then the other. "I was waiting for *him*, my dear, you know, like the letter said. Then all of a sudden I seemed to be surrounded with flames. But perhaps he is now here. Is it you, my dashing friend?" Game as ever, Lady Emmeline leered awfully at one of the young officers who had helped to extinguish the flames.

"Must be the shock. Addled her wits," muttered the officer.

Lord Varleigh arrived with Lady Jane on his arm. "Come, Miss Quennell," he said, "and I will assist you home."

But Annabelle had recognised the familiar figure of Captain MacDonald who had returned from changing his clothes.

"It's all right," she said. "Jimmy will look after me."

The Captain looked surprised and gratified at the familiar use of his Christian name. "Besides," added Annabelle sweetly to Lord Varleigh, "you must be very busy with your own concerns."

The Captain was already helping Lady Emmeline towards the door. Annabelle tripped quickly after them before Lord Varleigh could think of anything to say.

"Little cat," shrugged Lady Jane. "But I wish I knew the name of her dressmaker."

At the house in Berkeley Square Lady Emmeline was helped to bed and a footman dispatched to bring the doctor. Annabelle gave the Captain a hurried "good night" and quickly bobbed her head so that his kiss landed on the top of her hair.

In the privacy of her room she sat down to compose a long letter to her sisters.

Mary, the seventeen-year-old, would want to hear about the gentlemen; Susan, fifteen, must hear about the jewels; and Lisbeth, the ten-year-old, would want to hear all about the food Annabelle had eaten, particularly the sweets.

There must be nothing in the letter to excite the ready envy of her sisters. On the other hand they would be fearfully disappointed if it were dull. She did not mention her engagement. It all seemed so unreal. Perhaps some miracle would happen in the next few days and both Aunt Emmeline and the Captain would come to their senses. She would leave the matter for at least two days, and then write to her father and explain how it had all come about.

As she was preparing for bed, she remembered she was to attend a breakfast in the company of her fiancé the following afternoon. Horley had indicated that she should wear a sea-green silk gown which bore the hallmarks of all Madame Croke's depraved ingenuity. The wearer would leave little to the beholder's imagination. Annabelle bit her lip in vexation as she held it up to the candlelight. Then she remembered a package of lace curtains in the bottom drawer of a closet in the powder room. She brought them out of hiding, fetching her work basket, and began carefully and surely to snip and stitch until the sea green gown was covered in a delectable lace overdress with long prim sleeves.

She thought briefly of Lady Emmeline as she stitched away busily. Her godmother had escaped with only a few minor burns. It was almost as if the letter had been a deliberate ruse to entice the Dowager Marchioness into a trap. Shaking her head over her lurid fantasies, Annabelle finally snuffed out the candles and went to bed.

Chapter Four

ANNABELLE ENTERED HER godmother's bed-chamber late the following morning. At first she thought Lady Emmeline was dead. The waxy face on the pillow was bound tightly in bandages passing under the chin and ending in a bow on the top of her head. Her blond curls hung on a wig stand in the corner. Every available flat surface of the room was crammed with phials and bottles and boxes of creams and oils and unguents. A large gray and scarlet parrot wiped his beak against the bars of his cage and looked Annabelle over with all the hauteur of a patroness of Almack's.

The room was stiflingly hot. Lady Emmeline opened her eyes, saw Annabelle, and began to strip off her bandages.

"This is the best way to firm the chin," said that redoubtable old lady as soon as she could. "And stop staring at my face, child. 'Tis only oatmeal and water. The best cure for wrinkles there is."

Horley appeared like a grim shadow beside the bed. "Ah, Horley, hand me my hair," said Lady Emmeline as Annabelle tried not to stare at her hostess's shaven pate. "No, not the blond one, silly. 'Tis all smoke. I think the red will do to welcome my callers."

With all the expertise of a magician Horley popped a curly red wig on her mistress's head. "Now, fetch my chocolate and my appointments. I shall not be stirring today," said Lady Emmeline. "But there are engagements for Miss Quennell to fulfill. Ah, here we are. You and Jimmy are to attend the Standishes' breakfast. It is time you attended to your duties as a fiancée. Pray see that Jimmy does not drink too much. You will meet several of his fellow officers. Ah! how I envy you! When I remember the days . . . well, never mind."

In the short time before her departure for the Standishes' breakfast, Annabelle found herself worrying over the fact that she had not thanked Lord Varleigh for his gift of the novel. Would he be at the breakfast? Should she send him a letter by one of the footmen? A letter would perhaps be best.

A STRENGTHENING wind was pushing ominous-looking clouds across the sky when Lord Varleigh and Lady Jane Cherle arrived at the Standishes' imposing mansion at Henley. The crowd of guests bore witness to the fact that it was now easier to attend engagements out of town with the advent of faster and better sprung carriages and Macadam's hard, smooth-surfaced roads.

"They have surely room enough in that great barracks of a place to serve our food instead of pushing us into a drafty tent in the garden," pouted Lady Jane. The "drafty tent" was a smart red and white striped marquee capable of housing a hundred. "But then," went on Lady Jane, "Maria Standish always was an ambitious woman. You know, if I don't ask the Bloggs, then the Togs won't come, and if I don't ask the Fints, the Wints won't bring the Mints to meet the Bloggs and the Togs. Shall we go in? I am still shaking after last night. Of course, your brave little friend, Miss Quennell, plunged all unheeding into the smoke but then, some of these country-bred girls have no *sensibility*."

"And you have an excess of it," teased Lord Varleigh. Jane was wearing a flamboyant velvet gown in flaming scarlet which was intricately gored and flounced and ruched. She looked just like an elaborately wrapped Christmas present, he reflected with fond amusement. She had more than hinted the previous night that she wished to legalise their relationship, but as usual Lord Varleigh had shied away from the idea of marriage and had bought his mistress a magnificent rope of pearls by way of consolation. These now adorned Lady Jane's bosom, almost hidden in the multitude of tucks and frills.

Jane tugged at his arm and then looked up at Lord Varleigh in surprise. He was standing quite still, gazing across the lawns with an arrested look on his face. Jane followed his gaze. Annabelle Quennell was entering the gardens on the arm of Captain Jimmy MacDonald. Despite the chill of the day she only wore a silk shawl over her shoulders. The wind whipped at the lace overdress, sending it dancing and swirling round her body, revealing tantalising glimpses of the slim green dress underneath. She was wearing a frivolous little white straw bonnet with the brim lined with pleated green silk.

The Captain and his two cronies, Major Timothy Wilks and George Louch, appeared to be teasing Annabelle in a rather heavy manner for she suddenly blushed painfully and looked down at her shoes. Lord Varleigh was sorry for the girl. The Captain was a good sort, but there was no denying his humor was fit more for a tavern wench than for a gently bred girl. He would have started towards her had he suddenly not become aware of the vise-like grip on his arm. He looked down at his partner.

"I want to get out of this wind, Sylvester," she pouted prettily, "and you stand gawking at our country maiden."

Lord Varleigh felt himself becoming irritated by Lady Jane for the first time. Her possessive manner smacked more of the wife than the mistress.

Nevertheless he led Jane towards the marquee. It was arranged with flower-decorated tables, a long buffet with hundreds of delectable dishes, and in the center of them, in pride of place, the Standishes' enormous silver punch bowl. Most of the guests were already sampling the hot punch as the tent, like the day outside, was unseasonably cold.

Annabelle could only be glad that her fiancé had become engrossed in a conversation with his friends and had, for the moment, forgotten his heavy flirtatious manner.

The Captain and his friends seemed capable of betting on the most ludicrous things. The latest was a proposed cricket match to be held by the Greenwich pensioners, the eleven on one side to have but one arm each and both their legs; and the other to have both their arms and only one leg each. This strange match was to be run by a nobleman and a *would-be* member of the Jockey Club. The gentlemen were loudly debating whether to back the "legs" or the "wings" and roaring with noisy laughter at their own wit.

The talk of legs and the pressure against her own under the table made Annabelle wish Captain MacDonald would keep his own limbs to himself. No matter where she sat, he seemed to manage to press his legs against hers in the most embarrassing way. She suddenly felt his large hand on her knee and slapped it with the ivory sticks of her fan only to receive a reproachful look for her pains.

Annabelle was unaccustomed to liquor, and the two glasses of punch she had consumed had immediately gone to her head. She even began to find some of the Captain's jokes, which consisted of quite terrible puns, extremely funny and began to laugh very hard, wiping her streaming eyes with her lace handkerchief.

"Why, I believe they are well suited," said Lord Varleigh thoughtfully.

"Who?" said Jane impatiently. She did not like to be

interrupted when she was eating.

"Annabelle Quennell and her Captain."

"Oh, I am glad your mind is at rest," said Jane acidly and then murmured, "but I must find out the name of her dressmaker."

But Lord Varleigh had caught the undertone. He raised his quizzing glass. "Yes, Miss Quennell has a very individual style and a good sense of color," he remarked.

"Never mind her—have you heard the latest on-dit," said Jane. " 'Tis said, on Sunday two pairs of *turtle doves* took flight from Ingleton to Gretna Green; but by the nimble exertions of some *pouncing hawks*, the *cooing pair* were overtaken near Shap and very unpolitely conducted back to their respective homes!"

"If you mean young Honeywood and the Clermont girl, then why not say so?" said Lord Varleigh in a bored voice. "I detest the sleazy innuendo of the scandal sheet."

Lady Jane hunched a ruched, tucked, and embroidered velvet shoulder on him and began to talk loudly to a young man at the next table.

Lord Sylvester Varleigh found his gaze straying back to Annabelle. The girl was getting quite bosky and should not have been allowed on the Town with only Captain MacDonald as escort, affianced or not. But she had style, unusual in a girl unaccustomed to the intricate world of high fashion. Now Jane appeared most attractive in the bedchamber, after she had divested herself of her too elaborate toilette. He had a sudden vivid picture of Captain MacDonald and Annabelle in the bedchamber and shook his head to dispel the image.

Annabelle caught his glance in her direction, and the sudden look of distaste on his face, and sobered almost completely. She became aware that her face was flushed and that her hair was coming down at the back. The

Captain was interspersing his now very racy conversation with frequent demands for more punch. Annabelle remembered her godmother's warning and tugged at the Captain's braided sleeve. "Do you not think," she queried timidly, "that you have had enough to drink?"

The Captain gave her an outraged look, and his friends stared at her with their mouths open. "Had enough to drink?" echoed Mr. Louch in a high penetrating voice which carried round the marquee. "*Had enough to drink. Jimmy could drink that whole punch bowl and walk from here a sober man.*"

Annabelle looked at the punch bowl in amazement. It was the size of a young bath, made of solid silver and embellished with various embarrassing scenes from the Greek myths such as the Rape of Iphigenia.

"Hey, Captain," yelled an officer from the next table. "Lay you a monkey you couldn't do it."

"Done!" roared the Captain. He raced from the table and mounted to the buffet table by way of an empty chair, and before the cheering guests' eyes, he plunged headfirst into the punch bowl so that only his glossy Hessians could be seen waving in the air. A small tidal wave of punch slopped over the side and straight onto Lady Jane's lap. She began screaming and screaming while the guests roared and cheered. Lord Standish pushed his way through the crowd of the Captain's admirers to try to pull that gentleman from the punch bowl while Lady Standish led the now weeping Lady Jane towards the house to find her a change of clothes.

"By Jove, Miss Quennell!" howled George Louch exuberantly. "You're a lucky girl to have a man like that. What a capital gun!"

Am I too prim, thought Annabelle desperately? Why should I always feel so shocked and embarrassed? Everyone else seems to admire Captain MacDonald. Perhaps

I have not tried hard enough to understand him.

"It is time to go home, Miss Quennell." At the sound of the familiar voice Annabelle looked up and saw Lord Varleigh beside her chair. His normally hard gray eyes were warm with sympathy. Without a word she put her hand on his arm and they walked towards the entrance to the marquee. Annabelle turned back briefly. The Captain was sitting in the middle of the table with pieces of cinnamon and lemon in his hair like some exotic headdress. He had started to roar out a bawdy song and was being frantically hushed by Lord Standish. Then the Captain looked to where Annabelle was standing with Lord Varleigh, and his eyes suddenly looked very sober and alert. "Heh!" he cried. "Heh!" But Lord Varleigh had firmly led Annabelle from the marquee.

"I am afraid it is an open carriage," he said as they waited for the curricle to be brought round. "But I shall wrap you up in plenty of rugs."

Annabelle did not relax until they had left the Standish mansion well behind. She dreaded the Captain coming in pursuit of her. Perhaps Lord Varleigh dreaded being pursued by Lady Jane. To her horror she realised she had voiced this thought aloud, and Lord Varleigh glanced away from the management of his team to look at his companion with a certain tinge of amusement. "No, my dear Miss Quennell, I *am* the pursuer, I assure you. I shall be meeting Lady Jane again this evening so she will be quite content to exist without my company until then."

"Oh," said Annabelle, wondering why she felt a pang of disappointment. After all, it was not as if she wanted Lord Varleigh for herself. Or was it?

With a start she noticed they were turning into the courtyard of a smart posting inn and, for a moment, wild thoughts of abduction and seduction flew through her brain.

"Do not be afraid," said her companion, reading her mind with irritating ease. "I have just heard the noisy sounds of pursuit and feel sure you do not wish to meet your beloved in his present condition."

She eyed him doubtfully as he swung her down from his curricle. But then she heard unmistakable roars and tantivies coming closer on the road outside.

She peeped round the shelter of the curricle in time to see a smart phaeton, driven by the Captain, streaming past at a tremendous rate. Mr. Louch and Major Wilks were crammed on either side of him and hanging onto their tall hats for dear life. A slice of lemon rolled into the courtyard of the inn. The gallant Captain had obviously not waited to change.

Annabelle felt strangely embarrassed when she found herself seated alone with Lord Varleigh over the tea tray. But he settled comfortably back in his chair, entertaining her with an easy flow of conversation until she relaxed.

At last he said, "You must forgive the impertinence of the question, Miss Quennell, but is your proposed marriage with Captain MacDonald an *arranged* one? There does not seem to be much regard on either side."

"More tea?" queried Annabelle sweetly.

Lord Varleigh's thin brows snapped together, and then he laughed. Of course the very correct Miss Quennell would not discuss her engagement. He also longed to ask her why she had worn such an outrageously indecent gown to the opera but felt sure she would simply give him another setdown.

But Annabelle had thought of a safe topic of conversation. Had Lord Varleigh received her note of thanks for the book he had sent her? Indeed he had. He was amused to learn it was the first novel she had read.

"Mama would *never* allow me to read a novel," said Annabelle, "although she always insisted I was reading romances on the sly. Miss Austen's book seems all that is proper. Now the tales of the ancient Greeks are some-times *very* scandalous, but Mama never objected to those."

"Which translations did you read?" asked Lord Varleigh, noticing that Annabelle had an intriguing dimple in her cheek when she smiled.

"Oh, I read them in the original," said Annabelle blithely, unaware of Lord Varleigh's start of surprise. "Papa is a great scholar. I have been fortunate in my education. Oh, I had forgot. Godmother told me not to mention books in the presence of any member of the *haut ton* in case I was labelled a blue stocking."

"There is no fear of that. You are too beautiful," said Lord Varleigh simply and then cursed himself. His compliment had the effect of causing a closed, tight look on Annabelle's face, and she began to look at the clock with obvious impatience.

"Come," he teased. "I will take you home. But you must get in the way of receiving compliments, Miss Quennell. With your face and figure . . ." He allowed his eyes to roam insolently over her. To his surprise she did not blush or simper but stood looking at him with thinly veiled impatience.

"If you have finished taking your inventory, may I suggest we leave," snapped Annabelle. "And may I also suggest, my lord, that you save your intimate glances for Lady Jane Cherle!"

THE Dowager Marchioness was in a tearing fury, and the reason for her bad temper had not yet arrived home. She had sustained a visit from Captain MacDonald who had complained bitterly that Annabelle was causing no end of talk by leaving the breakfast with Lord Varleigh. The Captain was obviously "well to go" as he himself would have put it, and Lady Emmeline unfairly thought Annabelle had been encouraging him to drink, or at the very least keeping insufficient control of him.

She promised the Captain she would deal with her goddaughter when Annabelle arrived home and sent him packing. She was fully recovered from her fright of the night before and felt the need to take some action. Calling for Horley, she informed that long-suffering lady's maid that they were going out for a promenade and told her to take that look off her face and fetch the umbrella immediately.

For the hundredth time Lady Emmeline vowed to buy herself a new umbrella. Her old one was heavy and cumbersome but, for all that, seemed nigh indestructable. Heavy scarlet silk covered tough iron spokes and the umbrella felt as if it weighed a ton.

As she stood on her doorstep, several heavy spots of rain began to fall, driven by the rapidly increasing force of the wind, a fact that Horley pointed out with a sort of gloomy relish. But Lady Emmeline was determined to exercise. Exercise cleaned the liver and purged the bowels, she told Horley. She also remarked that Horley's perpetual long face was due to the disorder of her spleen.

Feeling slightly refreshed after this lecture, Lady Emmeline unfurled her enormous umbrella and stepped briskly out onto the pavement . . . and straight into— what appeared to the terrified Horley—to be an absolute rain of bricks. Bricks fell from the heavens like the thunderbolts of Jove and smashed down on her ladyship's doughty umbrella. The Dowager Marchioness was knocked to the ground by the weight of the bricks and fell screaming onto the pavement—unhurt, thanks to her umbrella—but terrified out of her wits.

It was at that moment that Annabelle arrived home, just in time to see the extraordinary sight of her godmother lying flat out on the pavement in a pile of bricks with her dress indecently hitched up, displaying her fat little calves bulging over a tight pair of glacé kid half boots. Lord Varleigh helped the shaken lady to her feet, and Lady Emmeline's wrath erupted.

"How dare you, sirrah," she roared in Lord Varleigh's surprised face. "My goddaughter is *affianced—affianced* d'ye hear?—to Captain MacDonald, and I will not have her traipsing around the countryside with a man who is little better than a *rake*."

"Control yourself," said Lord Varleigh coldly.

"And *you*," went on Lady Emmeline, rounding on Annabelle, "you ungrateful *baggage*. I bring you to London. I arrange a marriage for you with the finest young man . . ."

"That money can buy," said Annabelle, nearly as furious as her godmother.

"Don't be impertinent," roared the Dowager Marchioness, oblivious of the gathering crowd of spectators. "If I have any more of your nonsense, you will be packed back to Yorkshire in disgrace and not one penny of my money will you see."

"Your money cannot buy everything," shouted Annabelle, pink with mortification.

"Quite right," roared Lady Emmeline. "It can't buy poverty."

The avidly listening crowd cheered this sally, and Lady Emmeline's wrath fled like the black clouds above.

"Well, well," she said mildly. "Come into the house—you too, Varleigh. We should not be bandying words in public."

Begrimed with brick dust and with her bonnet and red wig askew, Lady Emmeline led the way into the house.

"What on earth happened to you, Lady Emmeline?" asked Lord Varleigh, holding open the door of the drawing room for her.

"Strangest thing," said Lady Emmeline, plopping herself down on the sofa. "Bricks—great whopping bricks—came falling out of the sky. I'd better send a man up to check the chimney stack. See to it, Horley. And as for you, Varleigh," she went on without checking for breath, "I'm sorry I let off at you like that. What exactly happened? Jimmy said you just upped and offed with Annabelle."

Lord Varleigh told her of the episode of the punch bowl, and Lady Emmeline laughed appreciatively. "What a man!" she gasped when she could. "Course, now I see you did the right thing, Varleigh, and I'm grateful to you. Jimmy's a good lad. He'll calm down once he's married." She rang for the butler and demanded that the brandy decanter be brought in, and Annabelle judged from the disapproving height of the butler's eyebrows that this was an unusual request.

Annabelle wondered what Mrs. Quennell would say if she could see her eldest daughter, the hope of the family, sitting quaffing brandy in the company of an elderly lady covered in brick dust and an aristocratic lord whose heart was well known to belong to one of the most dashing matrons of the Town.

Horley soon came back to inform the startled party that the chimney stack had been found intact but that there were signs someone had been hiding up on the roof for, it seemed, the sole purpose of throwing bricks at Lady Emmeline should she leave her mansion.

Lord Varleigh sat very still, his glass halfway to his lips, Annabelle was remembering Mad Meg's prophecy and feeling shaken, but Lady Emmeline only gave her infuriating giggle. "Why," she said, "I vow it was nothing more than some Tom or Jerry up there for a lark."

Annabelle had to admit that the Tom and Jerry sportsmen of the well-known cartoons were very close to real life. Was it strange that someone should throw bricks at an elderly dowager in a world where dropping live coals on a sleeping person and stealing a blind man's dog were considered the veriest demonstration of Corinthian high spirits?

Lord Varleigh rose to take his leave. He bowed punctiliously over Annabelle's hand, but his thoughts seemed to be elsewhere. Lady Emmeline had started to berate Horley over nothing in particular and everything in general, and Annabelle could not resist moving to the window to watch Lord Varleigh leave.

A smart yellow landau came to a stop in front of him. Smiling alluringly at Lord Varleigh from the landau was Lady Jane Cherle. A pale shaft of sunlight shone on the magnificent pearls at her throat. Lord Varleigh joined her in the carriage, and Lady Jane rested her head on his shoulder as they drove off.

Annabelle stood very still. Lady Jane had looked so sophisticated and beautiful. Annabelle became aware that she was engulfed in a new strong violent emotion. She wanted to see Lady Jane ruined; she wanted all London to laugh at her. Above all, Annabelle wanted Lord Varleigh to look at his mistress with contempt instead of with that heart-wrenching lazy intimacy.

I'm jealous, thought poor Annabelle. I'm jealous of Lady Jane's beauty. What a stupid wretch I am!

She raised her hands to her suddenly hot cheeks. Was this then how her sisters felt? With a new understanding of Mary, Susan, and Lisbeth tucked away in the Hazeldean rectory, Annabelle removed to her room to write a new kind of letter to them—telling them how much she missed them and how she longed to be home again.

Chapter Five

IN THE FOLLOWING days Annabelle became more and more accustomed to the bewildering social round.

Some of it seemed delightful, like the breakfasts among the Middlesex meadows or Surrey woods, and some, downright ridiculous. How on earth could one call an event a party when there was no room to sit, no conversation, no cards and no music—only shouting and elbowing through a succession of rooms meant to hold six hundred instead of the sixteen hundred invited? And then battling down the stairs again and the long wait for the carriage to make its way through the press so that one spent more time with the gold-laced footmen on the steps outside than with one's hosts upstairs.

Annabelle was to have her voucher for Almack's since Lady Emmeline was a great social power and any girl making a come-out under her aegis *must* be good *ton*.

In 1765 a Scotsman called William Macall reversed the syllables of his name to provide a more memorable title for his new Assembly Rooms—Almack's. Now nearly fifty years later at the height of its fame with a great wave of snobbery sweeping London, it thrived under the management of the haughty, vulgar, and indefatigable beauty, Lady Jersey. Not to have a voucher to one of Almack's Wednesday nights was to be damned socially and forever. So formidable were the patronesses that one of them, the Countess Lieven, was heard to say, "It is not fashionable where I am not."

51

A lady of the *ton* was expected to be fragile and useless and infinitely feminine. But the definition of a gentleman was the exact opposite, Annabelle learned. "An out and outer, one up to everything, down as a nail, a trump, a Trojan . . . one that can patter flash, floor a charley, mill a coal heaver, come coachey in prime style, up to every rig and row in town and down to every move upon the board from a nibble at the club to a dead hit at a hell; can swear, smoke, take snuff, lush, play at all games, and throw over both sexes in different ways—he is the finished man!" No wonder, reflected poor Annabelle, that Lady Emmeline was increasingly amazed that her strange goddaughter had not tumbled head over heels in love with Captain MacDonald.

But it *was* sometimes exciting, particularly in the evenings from six to eight and from eight to ten when Mayfair came alive with the rumbling of carriages, their flaming lamps twinkling along the fashionable streets, past tall houses ablaze with lights from top to bottom. And the food! Périgord pie and truffles from France, sauces and curry powder from India, hams from Westphalia and Portugal, caviar from Russia, reindeer tongues from Lapland, olives from Spain, cheese from Parma, and sausages from Bologna.

Sometimes the sheer extravagance of the members of this gilded society seemed overwhelming to Annabelle. Lady Londonderry went to a ball so covered in jewels that she could not stand and had to be followed around with a chair. And her very handkerchiefs cost fifty guineas the dozen. Everything, as the Corinthians would say, had to be "prime and bang up to the mark."

Despite various discreet requests Annabelle had refused to divulge the name of her dressmaker for fear Madame Croke would discover Annabelle's alterations to her styles.

To her disappointment she had not yet found a female friend. In the hurly-burly of the marriage mart she was marked down as one of the few who had already succeeded. Members of her own sex who were still out there on the battleground preferred to huddle together in groups, plotting and exchanging gossip.

London was enjoying an unusually fine spell of hot weather so it was possible to wear the delicate lawns and Indian muslins without also displaying acres of mottled gooseflesh. Annabelle was to attend a fête champêtre on-board the Hullocks' "little yacht." Mr. Hullock was a wealthy merchant who entertained the *ton* lavishly in the hope of securing titled marriages for his daughters. But the aristocracy drank his fine French vintages and guzzled his food and remained as aloof and patronising as ever.

A long box had arrived from Madame Croke containing Annabelle's costume for the party. In vain had Annabelle pleaded with Lady Emmeline to be allowed to make her own. What could a country miss know of fashion, Lady Emmeline had demanded.

Annabelle stared at the contents of the box in dismay. Madame Croke had surpassed herself. A neat label in tight script declared it to be the costume of Athene. It was of fine white lawn—so fine it was nigh transparent and the skirt ended *just below the knee.* Did Madame Croke expect Annabelle to show her legs in public? She obviously did.

Annabelle recalled having seen a slim rose silk gown in her vast wardrobe. With a few tucks and changes and stitches, it could be transformed into an alluring underdress. The flounces at the hem would have to be removed to style the dress in keeping with the Greek-goddess image.

The gold helmet was, however, very flattering and

no doubt Monsieur André, the hairdresser, would twist Annabelle's long curls into an attractive style to suit it.

She bent her head over the costume and began to work.

Horley came into the room as quietly as a shadow. Annabelle guiltily thrust her work behind her. "What is it, Horley?" she demanded as Horley's piercing black eyes seemed to stare straight through her to the costume hidden behind.

"It's the Captain, miss. Captain MacDonald," said Horley, holding open the door and stepping aside to let Annabelle past. "He's waiting downstairs."

"I shall be down presently," said Annabelle. "And next time, please knock, Horley."

"Good servants *never* knock," said Horley righteously.

"Then scratch at the door. You know exactly what I mean, Horley," snapped Annabelle. Horley bristled with anger and then turned abruptly and left the room.

She was quite sure miss was tampering with those gowns and more than one lady had held out a bribe to Horley in the hopes of finding out the name of Annabelle's dressmaker. Then they should have it, decided Horley grimly, and that might give that little upstart something to worry about.

The Captain was pacing up and down the room. He stopped when he saw Annabelle, and the pair went through their peculiar hit-and-miss ballet—the Captain trying to kiss Annabelle and Annabelle trying to avoid the kiss being planted on her mouth. At last the Captain turned to the decanter as usual and, after he had poured himself a generous measure of canary, he asked Annabelle in a surprisingly gentle voice if she would mind if he did not escort her to the fête.

Annabelle did not mind in the least but felt it would be rude to say so. She compromised by pointing out that

54

the Captain had indeed been a dutiful escort during the previous days and that she felt he deserved an "evening off."

The Captain beamed at her with affectionate relief. There was a prime mill at Brick Hill and he would not miss it for worlds and if he did not get there the night before, then he would not be able to command the best place since sportsmen from all over the country would be journeying there. He waxed almost poetical on the subject of boxing—how the last time he had been at Brick Hill, he had been loitering around the inn door when a barouche and four had driven up with Lord Byron and a party and Jackson, the trainer. How they had all dined together and how marvellous it had been, the intense excitement, the sparring, then the first round and— oh! it was . . . *Homeric*.

Annabelle smiled and tried not to show her relief at the prospect of a social evening without the Captain.

LADY Jane Cherle bit her rather full underlip. For all Lord Varleigh's kisses and caresses, she had not liked the way he had promptly walked off with Annabelle from the Standishes' breakfast. He had just now sent Jane a note saying that he would be grateful if she could make her own way to the Hullocks' party as he had some pressing business. She would not go, thought Jane pettishly. But her costume of a Turkish harem girl was infinitely seductive, and she did not want its charms to go to waste. After some thought she decided she would go after all—but very, very late. That would give Sylvester Varleigh time to miss her. And that way she could make a very splendid last minute appearance.

ANNABELLE and Lady Emmeline were late by the time they boarded the Hullocks' enormous yacht which was moored in the Thames near to Vauxhall Gardens. The decks of the yacht were thickly carpeted in oriental rugs, and silk canopies fluttered over the heads of the guests. A magnificent red sunset was blazing through the forest of masts of the other ships.

Mr. Hullock was as proud and as pleased with his fashionable guests as if they were a friendly company of kindred spirits instead of a vacuous-faced jostling throng. As darkness crept over the water and young Rossini's music serenaded the guzzling guests, Annabelle noticed Lord Varleigh climbing aboard. He was correct to an inch in formal evening dress instead of costume; chapeau bras and knee breeches, ruffled shirt and cravat, short jacket with swallow tails, diamonded pumps and dress sword. His gaze wandered towards Annabelle, he gave a brief smile, and then continued to search the crowd. He is looking for Lady Jane, thought Annabelle. Her costume which had seemed so dashing and alluring only a few minutes ago now seemed to poor Annabelle to have become downright frumpish. Her head sank slightly under her gold helmet, and she stared dismally at the dirty water moving beside the schooner.

When she raised her head again, it was to see that Lord Varleigh had given up his search for Lady Jane and was moving towards her. All of a sudden Annabelle did not want to be singled out as second best. She moved swiftly away towards the stern of the ship where the light of the many lanterns did not reach.

The heartbreaking strains of a waltz echoed in the still air, and the smells of wine and French cooking mingled with the less attractive smells of the river.

As her eyes grew accustomed to the gloom, Annabelle could make out the shapes of a couple approaching her. She shrank back into the blackness and stood very still, not wanting her confused thoughts to be interrupted.

It was then she realised that the couple were approaching in a very odd manner. With surprise, she made out the gold lace of Lady Emmeline's evening gown, the Dowager Marchioness having decided not to go in costume.

But Lady Emmeline was walking *backwards*, and instead of accompanying her, the gentleman was behind her. A sudden burst of fireworks went up from Vauxhall Gardens and Annabelle noticed with horror that Lady Emmeline's escort or pursuer was dressed as a pirate and was carrying a very lethal-looking cutlass which he was pointing straight at the terrified Dowager Marchioness.

"Back," grated the "pirate" in a hoarse voice. His face was masked and his eyes glittered strangely through the slits in the black velvet. "Over the side with you," he hissed, holding the point of the cutlass dangerously near the terrified Lady Emmeline's throat.

"I c-can't s-swim," babbled Lady Emmeline. "I sh-shall drown."

"Exactly," mocked the pirate.

"Wait!" cried Annabelle, darting forward. She stood in front of her terrified godmother. "Now, my man," she said, "you have two of us to deal with."

"Get out of the way, you silly little *doxy*," rasped the pirate. Annabelle felt the point of the cutlass at her throat, but she did not flinch. Annabelle would have been very surprised indeed had she been told she was being extremely brave. Her duty was to rescue her godmother at all costs.

Her mind worked very quickly. Her godmother's attacker obviously wanted Lady Emmeline's death to look like an accident. Then she must risk screaming for help.

She threw back her head and screamed as loudly as she could, and great shriek upon shriek echoed along the length of the vessel.

There came the sound of running footsteps as Lord Varleigh hurtled along the companionway, his drawn sword in his hand. The pirate looked from Annabelle to Lord Varleigh and jumped nimbly over the side of the schooner. There was a loud splash. Annabelle craned her head over the side. There came another burst of golden stars from the Vauxhall fireworks, and she could see the pirate's head bobbing among their golden reflections as he swam with strong strokes to the shore.

More people came running up, and there was a tremendous babble of "What happened" and "Good gracious" and the high voice of Mr. Louch suggesting, "It might have been Harry Stokes. *He's* dressed as Neptune and mayhap wants some more fair maidens for his kingdom. Oh! 'Tis Lady Emmeline. Then he is perhaps in the need of *some old trout*."

"Shame," cried several voices, and Mr. Louch, who was dressed as a rajah, retired in disorder.

The Countess Honeyford, an old friend of Lady Emmeline, who was finding the entertainments tiresome and had complained bitterly at having been introduced to a mere merchant before she had taken two aristocratic steps on board, offered to escort the shaken Dowager Marchioness home.

Lady Emmeline recovered enough to give Annabelle a warm hug. "You saved my life, my dear," she said clasping Annabelle to her scanty bosom. "No need for you to rush away. Look after her, Varleigh, will you?"

"Delighted," said Lord Varleigh smoothly, leading Annabelle away. Annabelle wondered why she stayed. It was surely her duty to go home with Lady Emmeline. As she and Lord Varleigh elbowed and pushed their way through the throng, hands caught at Lord Varleigh's sleeve and mocking voices asked him what he had done with Lady Jane. Annabelle saw the plump figure of her godmother being helped down into a small boat which was to take her to the farther shore and made an impulsive move to run after her but found herself restrained by the surprising strength of Lord Varleigh's fingers.

Bowing and smiling to his acquaintances, he led the reluctant Annabelle to a quiet corner, picking up a bottle of champagne and two glasses on the way.

"Now, my delectable Athene," he said, filling her glass. "You must tell me exactly what happened."

As he listened carefully to her story, he was touched and amused by the bravery she had displayed and by the fact that she was completely unaware of it.

When she had finished, he sat in silence for what seemed to Annabelle a very long time. At last he said, "Someone is trying to kill Lady Emmeline."

Annabelle had already come to just that conclusion herself, but it was shocking to hear it voiced in such a quiet conversational tone. "What are we to do?" she asked.

"Keep a close guard on her," he said, "and watch for anyone who might be her enemy. I shall help you, Miss Quennell."

"Thank you," said Annabelle quietly, stealing a shy look at his profile. He turned suddenly and smiled down at her, and she felt as if her bones had turned to water.

Most of the guests were leaving and many of the lanterns had burned out. But in the dim light he could see Annabelle's large eyes searching his own and the faint tremor of her lips. On impulse he bent his head and placed a fleeting kiss on her mouth. The young soft lips beneath his seemed to cling and burn, and he raised his head and stared at her in silence as the shrill voice of his mistress cut through the chatter of the departing guests, "Sylvester! Has anyone seen Sylvester?"

Lord Varleigh took Annabelle's hand in his and held

it. "Not tonight," he murmured. "No. Not tonight, Lady Jane."

Lady Jane stood surrounded by the remainder of the guests. "Varleigh's gone off with that Quennell girl," came the high voice of George Louch. "MacDonald will have something to say about *that*," he added with a titter.

Lady Jane's large eyes seemed to bore into the darkness where Annabelle was sitting. For a moment her face was white with fury and then, in an instant, she had changed to her usual coquettish self.

"Then who will be my cavalier?" she cried. Several male voices answered in assent, and surrounded by a laughing and cheering group, Lady Jane departed.

Annabelle became aware that Lord Varleigh was still holding her hand and tugged it free. She was suddenly hot with shame at the enormity of her behavior. What on earth would her father say were he to know that she had let one man kiss her while she was engaged to another?

But Lord Varleigh rose and collected his chapeau bras and escorted Miss Quennell home as if nothing at all had passed between them. She did not know whether to be angry or glad.

To Annabelle's surprise Lady Emmeline was waiting up for her. Lord Varleigh had left Annabelle on her doorstep to go . . . where? To Lady Jane? Or did the "No, not tonight" still apply?

Lady Emmeline was dressed more in keeping with her age in a faded kimono and as a result looked considerably younger.

"Come in, sit down, my dear," she said as Annabelle entered. "I have not yet thanked you enough for saving my life." She raised one plump, beringed hand as Annabelle would have protested. "No, indeed! It was a most courageous action. You have more spirit than . . .

than . . . well, than I would ever have guessed. You must tell me what I can give you. Jewels? Furs . . . no, not the season. Come now. There must be something you want?"

"You have given me enough, Godm . . . I mean, Emmeline," said Annabelle slowly, "but there is just one thing . . ."

"Which is?"

Annabelle clasped her suddenly trembling hands together in her lap. She looked straight at her godmother. "I do not wish to be affianced to Captain MacDonald," she said.

Lady Emmeline's eyes fell before the girl's direct look. "Well, well, well," she said. "Tol rol. It's your inexperience, girl. If you knew more of the ways of men, then you would appreciate a fine upstanding man like the Captain."

She looked hopefully at Annabelle who said firmly, "I really mean it, you know. I do not wish to marry Captain MacDonald."

"Umph!" said Lady Emmeline sulkily. Then her wrinkled, monkey face took on a crafty look under its mask of powder and paint. "Then so be it. I shall send a notice that your engagement is at an end to the newspaper in the morning. Do not trouble to speak to Captain MacDonald yourself. I shall see him for you."

"Oh, *thank you* . . . ," Annabelle was beginning when Lady Emmeline interrupted her. "But the poor Captain is quite smitten with you, you know. I mean, it would not be fair to drop him *entirely*, heh? No harm in him escorting you here and there till you're suited. After all, your papa would not want you to do anything rash. Seems to me he's quite pleased about it." She drew a crumpled letter from the sleeve of her kimono.

The rector had written to Lady Emmeline stating his joy and delight that Annabelle was already engaged. He went on at some length on the subject. Annabelle's eyes were misted over with tears as she handed it back, and Lady Emmeline could only be glad that the girl had not noticed the missing sheet of the letter where the rector had then set out all his anxieties and hopes that it was a marriage of the *heart*.

"So you'll try?" queried Lady Emmeline, her sharp eyes watching the girl's expressive face. "Just to please a poor old woman."

Annabelle nodded dumbly.

Lady Emmeline's eyes suddenly narrowed like those of a large tabby cat. "Ah, Varleigh, now. He escorted you home?"

"Yes," said Annabelle a little breathlessly and felt the guilty color beginning to mantle her cheeks.

"Well, there's a triumph! Of course," went on Lady Emmeline smoothly, "there has from time to time been some pretty debutante who has managed to pry my lord from Lady Jane's side. But not for long. He only does it to make her jealous. Oh well"—here she gave a fake yawn—"I suppose that pair will be tying the knot before long. London's ceased being scandalized at their affair. God knows, it's been going on long enough!"

And having noticed that the barb had gone home, Lady Emmeline took herself off to bed.

But after Horley had snuffed the candles and Lady Emmeline lay abed in the dark listening to the wind in the trees outside and the high monotonous call of the watch, she began to turn over the events of the evening in her mind. She should never have left the girl alone with Varleigh. He had not been with Lady Jane for long, and it looked as if he would not be with her for much longer, but she certainly wasn't going to let Miss Annabelle Quennel know *that*! She then thought of her assailant. Could someone be trying to kill her? Fiddlesticks! Who could want to? Probably I'm the target of some mad bet, thought Lady Emmeline sleepily. They'll find something else to bet on, on the morrow. She was suddenly very tickled at the idea that her name might be appearing at this very moment in White's betting book.

As for the Captain, she would tell him to play things easily. Annabelle was too shy and country bred to appreciate someone like the Captain. She needed some town bronze. Let her cancel the engagement. She would be engaged to the Captain again before the Season was out. He was just like his father, thought Lady Emmeline dreamily. Captain MacDonald's father had been her one and only love. Unfortunately she had been married to the Marquess at the time or perhaps Captain Jimmy MacDonald might have been her own son.

Annabelle should come about. All it needed was a bit of plotting and careful handling. Damn Varleigh! Why did he have to start poking his long nose into her affairs . . .

Chapter Six

"WHAT THE *hell* is going on?" demanded Captain MacDonald two days later. He had stayed on at Brick Hill to enjoy the roistering after the prize fight, and the first he knew of the end of his engagement was when he saw it staring up at him in black and white from the sheets of his morning paper.

"Damme," he said wrathfully. "Can't you control that girl?"

"Quiet down and listen," said Lady Emmeline, admiring the Captain's handsome figure. "We rushed the girl, you know. Handle her gently and she'll come about."

"Why *Annabelle*" demanded the Captain wrathfully. "Lots of other gels would be glad to have me."

"I'm sure of it," said Lady Emmeline soothingly. "But my late sister, Caroline, was fond of Annabelle's mother. Poor Caroline was always fretting about the Quennells and when she knew she was dying, she made me promise to help them. And so I shall. I'm fond of you, Jimmy, love you like a son, but a family promise is a family promise."

"But the gel won't get any money an' she marries someone else?" demanded the Captain.

"Don't know," said Lady Emmeline. "She saved my life, you know. I suppose it was all meant as a joke or some sort of wager, but I'd have died if I'd gone into that river."

"What on earth are you talking about?" demanded the Captain. "Has everyone gone *mad*?"

Lady Emmeline told him all about her adventure, and the Captain said nastily that he thought it sounded more like a production at the Haymarket Theatre, and then followed it up with a hearty laugh as he saw the clouds gathering on Lady Emmeline's wrinkled brow.

He started pacing up and down the room, his brow creased in thought. "Look! Let me talk to Annabelle and I'll put it right. I'll do what you say, of course. I won't rush my fences."

"Very well," said Lady Emmeline, touching the bell. "Send Miss Quennell down," she said to one of her many footmen who had answered the summons. "Do not say that Captain MacDonald is here. Merely say that I wish to see her."

And so it was that Annabelle, tripping lightly into the room some ten minutes later, found only the Captain, waiting beside the fireplace with one glossy Hessian boot propped on the fender and the inevitable glass of ruby red liquid in his hand.

She looked at him, blushing with embarrassment, but he merely smiled at her in a kindly way and said, "Don't take fright, Annabelle. I ain't going to eat you. I only want to say how sorry I am that our engagement is at an end."

"I am sorry to have caused you so much distress, sir," said Annabelle in a low voice.

"Oh, I'll be all right," said the captain cheerfully, "except, of course, that there ain't a war on, and I've become used to squiring a lady around. You won't mind if we stay friends, will you? Until you're suited, that is?"

Annabelle moved over to the window with her back to him and gazed out into the square. How was she to be expected to meet anyone else if she were to be constantly seen in the Captain's company?

But as she gazed into the square, a smart highflyer phaeton rolled past with Lord Varleigh at the reins and Lady Jane perched up behind him, laughing and holding on to a ridiculous little hat.

"Thank you," said Annabelle in a subdued voice and turning round. "That is very kind of you."

"Splendid," beamed the Captain. "Tell you what— run and fetch your bonnet and I'll take you for a drive. You haven't seen much of London apart from St. James's."

The sun shone in at the window. Everyone else who mattered seemed to be out there having a marvellous time.

Annabelle agreed and was ushered off the premises by an ecstatic Lady Emmeline.

"I know what I'll do," said Captain MacDonald when Annabelle was safely ensconsed beside him in the carriage. "I'll take you to all those places they show the country cousins. You'll like that."

Annabelle turned her head away to hide a smile. The Captain could not be said to be a model of tact.

To her surprise she found herself thrilled and surprised by her outing. They drove first to the middle of Westminster Bridge and stopped to look at the great green and gray river with its barges and wherries and brown sails. Upstream lay the terraced trees and houses in front of Westminster Hall, the new Millbank Penitentiary and the low, willowed banks, and downstream, the crumbling old taverns and warehouses of Scotland Yard.

Then they drove over the high-balustraded bridge, with its bays and hooped lampposts, to the Surrey shore. After a short depressing ride through rows of mean, small dwellings and dingy factories, they returned once more to the river and over the camelback of London Bridge where the river narrowed into cataracts and poured down through arches. And so into the City, the commercial hub.

Annabelle found it all bewilderingly unlike the quiet streets of the West End.

Postmen in scarlet coats with bells and bags mingled with porterhouse boys with pewter mugs. Bakers cried "Hot loaves," chimney sweeps with brushes, hawkers with bandboxes on poles, milkmaids with pails, all were crying their wares over the din made by the bells of the dust carts and the horns of the news vendors.

And the shops!

Windows were piled high with silks and muslin and calicoes, china and glassware, jewels and silver. Businessmen in broadcloth edged past children bowling hoops and workmen in aprons and padded leather jackets and raree-show men carrying the magic of their trade on their backs.

Annabelle stared openmouthed as they bowled across the wide cobbled expanse of Finsbury Square. Then across Old Street and past the gloomy facade of St. Luke's Hospital for the insane with its large figures of Melancholy and Raving Madness. And then a long way round by Islington and Pentonville, out to Hampstead and Highgate, back towards London past the Yorkshire Stingo Pleasure Gardens at Lisson Grove and Mr. Lord's cricket ground—now scheduled for building—and along the Edgeware Road where Annabelle at last recognised the wooden Tyburn turnpike and the northern wall of Hyde Park.

All through the journey the Captain kept up a light easy flow of conversation. Annabelle found she had enjoyed her day and was no longer afraid that the Captain would subject her to an *excess of civility*. And nor did he. Instead of trying to kiss her, he merely bent punctiliously over her hand and said he hoped to see her at the opera.

Annabelle found Lady Emmeline bubbling over with the latest on-dit. The Russian Czar, Alexander, as a member of the coalition who had defeated Napoleon, was visiting London. The latest was that the great Czar fancied himself in love with Lady Jersey and now Almack's was most definitely more fashionable than Carlton House since the Prince Regent's unpopularity with his subjects had become a byword.

And the bliss of it all, went on Lady Emmeline, was that no one, but no one, had even *noticed* the cancellation of Annabelle's engagement. They had now such a juicy piece of gossip to chew on.

Annabelle felt unaccountably depressed. She wondered if Lord Varleigh had read his morning paper or if he, too, had been too taken up with the latest on-dit to notice it.

THE Haymarket Theatre was crammed to its flame-colored dome when Annabelle and Lady Emmeline took their places in their box that evening. All the other boxes were filled, row after row with women in white satin gowns and diamonds and men in orders and gold lace. Catalani, that famous singer, began to drown out the noise of both chorus and orchestra with her well-known piercing voice. It was some time, therefore, before Annabelle realised that the Captain had entered and was sitting quietly in the corner, his face shielded from the light by one of the red curtains. A very ripe aroma exuded from him which seemed to be made up of various liqueurs and vast quantities of snuff.

Annabelle eyed him warily, but he was leaning forward now with his head resting on his hand, apparently absorbed in Catalani's caterwauling.

Suddenly he said something. Annabelle could not quite make out what he had said but understood it to be some comment on the music.

The Captain's voice rose and whatever he had said before, he said louder again, but Catalani's voice had risen also at precisely the same time.

Annabelle turned in some irritation and raised her eyes in a manner which would have pleased Lady Emmeline's butler.

"I SAID, 'I LOVE YOU!'" roared the Captain.

The music from both orchestra and singers had unfortunately reached a lull, and the Captain's words rang round the theater. Everyone giggled and stared and several of his cronies, recognising the Captain, sent up a cheer.

"Please, keep your voice down," whispered poor Annabelle.

"I LOVE YOU!" shouted the Captain like a war cry, and his great voice echoed round the theater. How the audience roared and hooted and cheered and how the drunken Captain loved it. He had completely forgotten about Annabelle and was now performing his own interpretation of a Highland fling on the parapet of the box.

Annabelle tried to appeal to Lady Emmeline for help, but that infuriating old eccentric was laughing until the tears streamed down her rouged cheeks. Annabelle began to think they were all mad. If a lady made the slightest indiscretion, it was all over London the next day, and the doors of Almack's were firmly barred to her. But a gentleman, it seemed, could behave like a drunken lout and still be considered "the finished man."

The performers on stage were continuing as if nothing had happened.

Suddenly there was a stir in one of the boxes along

the row from Annabelle. Through the cavorting of the Captain's long limbs on the edge of the box, she could see a small gentleman with a beaky profile being welcomed by his friends.

The Captain saw the gentleman as well and the effect on him was electric. He bolted into the box like a rabbit into its burrow. Then the door at the back of the box slammed and he was gone.

"Who is that man?" said Annabelle, pointing with her fan.

"Oh, 'tis the Duke of Wellington," said Lady Emmeline. "I hope he did not see Captain MacDonald, or poor Jimmy will be receiving a dressing down from his colonel in the morning."

Annabelle was thankful to learn that there appeared to be some law and order in the higher ranks of the British army. The aristocrats who made up most of the ranks of officers seemed to treat their military service as if it was some sport akin to fox hunting and, during peacetime, hardly ever appeared in uniform except during the long ceremonial parades for the Czar's visit.

How she wished she did not have to bear the antics of the embarrassing Captain! Her cheeks were hot with shame, and it was with some relief that she finally realised no one at all was bothering to look in her direction.

Annabelle had not, however, noticed that Lady Emmeline had been watching her closely. I have thrust her at the Captain too much, thought that wily old lady. Perhaps if I tell her she's free and can do as she pleases and make sure little Annabelle and her Captain are thrown together . . . why then . . . who knows what may happen?

From the darkness of his box Lord Varleigh studied Annabelle through his quizzing glass, finding the appearance she made more appealing than the sights on stage. Lady Jane Cherle followed his gaze and her heart sank. Whenever Lord Varleigh saw the Quennell female, his attention seemed to be immediately rivetted on her. Annabelle was everything that Lady Jane feared and despised—a beautiful and missish idiot who had never suffered from the cold breath of scandal. Well, perhaps that could be arranged. She had no intention of losing Sylvester Varleigh—even if she had to intrigue, or kill, to keep him.

As Annabelle and Lady Emmeline alighted from their carriage in Berkeley Square later that evening, Lady Emmeline paused on the pavement, her whole face looking very serious and intent in the flickering light of the flambeaux blazing outside her house. She dismissed the carriage and then clasped Annabelle's arm. "I am *enjoying* myself," said the old lady, the wind from the square blowing her flimsy dress against the bones of her corset, "and it's all thanks to you. Youth keeps you young," she went on, her eyes fastening almost greedily on Annabelle's fresh features. "You can marry who you like and when you like, my dear. You'll be a daughter to me. Yes, a daughter!"

Leaning heavily on the young girl, she moved into the house.

Unseen by either, a dark shadow detached itself from the railings a little way off down the street and slipped silently away to merge with the blacker shadows of the night.

Chapter Seven

LADY EMMELINE'S NEWFOUND delight in her goddaughter had not abated on the following morning, and she started to plan a ball to be held in Annabelle's honor.

The long ballroom which was at the back of the four-story house had not been used in years, and an army of servants was sent to dust and polish and scrub and take the Holland covers from the crystal chandeliers.

Madame Croke was sent for in order that a stupendous ball gown could be planned for Annabelle, who awaited the arrival of the dressmaker with some trepidation.

Annabelle conjured up a picture of Madame Croke as a hard-faced woman with snapping black eyes and the mannerisms of a demimondaine.

To her amazement Madame Croke was a small, faded, spinsterish woman with a small, faded voice. She was soberly dressed in a gray tweed pelisse worn over a gray Kerseymere wool dress. The severity of her bonnet would have graced the head of the sternest governess. It was hard to believe that this quiet mouse of a woman was capable of dreaming up some of the most outrageous toilettes in London. She had brought with her a folio of sketches for Annabelle to shudder over. Each gown looked more daring and scanty than the next.

When Annabelle at last arrived at a drawing of a simpering lady wearing little else other than jewel-be-decked gauze, she closed the folder firmly and said:

"These will not do, Madame Croke. They are more suitable for a member of the demimonde than for a debutante."

Lady Emmeline was busy entertaining the Countess Honeyford, and after giving the Dowager Marchioness a quick look, Madame Croke dropped her voice to a whisper. "Then perhaps, Miss Quennell," she murmured, handing Annabelle a pencil, "you might care to make a few alterations yourself? You see, so many ladies have come to me, asking me to design a gown exactly like the one Miss Quennell was wearing on such and such an occasion. I did not know what they were talking about, so I made the effort of watching you when you went out. I have built my reputation by creating, let us say, a rather *fast* line of creations. But perhaps, with your help, I could supply clothes to young ladies of quality like yourself. I should not, of course, be financially ungrateful if you were to give me some assistance."

Annabelle stared at the dressmaker in surprise and delight. The thought of earning her living in this bewildering world where a lady was not supposed even to stoop to retrieve her own handkerchief was a heady novelty. She was also thrilled at the thought of being able to send some money home.

"I shall begin right away," said Annabelle cheerfully. "I shall first sketch a suitable design for my ball gown and then, if you wish, I will suggest some more designs for gowns for other ladies. But please do not tell my godmother!"

Madame Croke shook her head and both bent over the designs, Annabelle's clever pencil flicking over the alterations.

When Annabelle at last raised her head, she felt she had finally achieved the ball gown of her dreams. It was to be made of white Indian muslin embroidered from neckline to hem with roses of gold silk thread. Tiny artificial gold roses were to decorate the line above the deep flounce at the hem, the neckline and the edges of the little puffed sleeves. A headdress of roses would be wound through her red-gold curls to complete the effect.

She could imagine the beautiful dress floating and swirling round her legs as she danced the steps of the waltz with . . . For a moment Lord Varleigh's thin white aristocratic face floated in her mind's eye. She resolutely banished it and replaced it with the square tanned face and merry eyes of her dream lover.

ANNABELLE'S ball was voted "a sad crush" which meant that it was one of the successes of the Season. Royalty did not attend but practically everyone else did, from the haughty Lady Jersey to the impeccable Mr. Brummell.

Many gentlemen seemed only too ready to overlook the fact that Miss Quennell had no fortune, although, as the evening wore on and the champagne flowed, some of them became too enthusiastic, and Annabelle found it necessary to cool their ardor by behaving like a very haughty young lady indeed—or by "getting stiffly on her stiffs" as the current slang had it.

The ballroom was as hot as Clarence House despite the fact that the long windows were open onto the dusty garden at the back.

Annabelle found herself sympathising with Mr. Hullock, the merchant. The aristocracy seemed to be using her ball as an extension of the marriage mart. They gave Annabelle vague kind smiles, and a few of the older members patted her cheek, but the female half of the guests discounted her as a whole—the gentlemen were much too interested in her and no one without a fortune should be as beautiful as that! Her glorious, healthy, voluptuous good looks were gradually damned as vulgar as the evening went on and all the best of the marriageable men showed an irritating tendency to be more attentive than they should be.

Lady Jersey deigned to hold Annabelle in conversation all through the first waltz, rattling on at a great rate, and Annabelle, whose feet itched to dance, although the waltz was still considered rather *fast*, wished heartily that this queen of London Society would go away. She felt inclined to agree with the irrepressible Princess of Wales—"Mein Gott, dat is de dullest person Gott Almighty ever did born!"

At last Lady Jersey twittered off having felt she had done her duty by noticing *dear* Lady Emmeline's tiresome goddaughter.

Lord Varleigh entered the ballroom and stood looking round the guests. Annabelle had begun to think he would not come, and it was with a queer little uplifting of the heart that she noticed that Lady Jane was not with him.

He came towards her, complimented her warmly on the elegance of her gown and then bent his head over her dance card. She hoped he would notice that the space opposite the next waltz had been left empty. She hoped Captain MacDonald would not come up at that moment and claim the waltz for himself. Certainly the Captain had been very subdued and attentive ever since his clowning at the opera. He had spent most of the ball in the card room but had made sudden forays into the ballroom between dances to stand next to Annabelle in an infuriatingly proprietorial way.

But Lord Varleigh merely scribbled his name opposite the waltz and stood chatting with her easily until her next partner came to claim her for the quadrille.

Lord Varleigh leaned against a pillar and watched Annabelle as she elegantly executed the steps of the dance. She had an almost fairy charm, he decided, with her beautiful creamy skin, red-gold hair, and air of fresh innocence. She appeared infinitely feminine and vulnerable, a girl to marry and cherish and protect. He realised with a little start that he had been thinking quite a lot of Miss Quennell lately and felt a strange pang of disappointment whenever he entered a party or ball and found her not there.

"Is that Lady Jersey's vulgar debutante?" asked Beau Brummell, appearing suddenly at Lord Varleigh's side. The famous Beau put up his quizzing glass and surveyed the dancing Annabelle.

"No, not vulgar . . . not vulgar at all," said Mr. Brummell, letting his quizzing glass fall. "She has style and freshness—she is an original—a veritable country rose blooming on this rocky and bitter London soil. Charming! I find her charming."

Lord Varleigh watched Brummell moving away with some amusement. That well-known London gossip, Jeffrey Roberts, had been listening avidly. Before much more of the evening had passed, Annabelle would be hailed as the new beauty. Such was the power of the Beau.

Soon she was floating in Lord Varleigh's arms in the steps of the waltz. Although he held her the regulation twelve inches away, he was disturbingly aware of her body swaying in his arms. When the dance finished, he found himself strangely reluctant to leave her. He asked her if she would like some refreshment and sent a footman to fetch two glasses of wine while he led her to a small sofa beside the open windows.

"You are looking very beautiful tonight," he said when they were seated together. "Charming, Brummell called you, and he is quite right."

Annabelle blushed with pleasure and turned a glowing

face to his. "Did he really say that?" she cried with ingenuous delight at the compliment.

"You are like a child with sweetmeats," laughed Lord Varleigh. "Are you not in the way of receiving compliments?"

"Oh, yes, lots," said Annabelle, "particularly this evening. But no one has ever called me charming before."

"You must become accustomed to hearing it," teased Lord Varleigh. "If the great Brummell says you are charming, then charming will be your label."

"Then I shall simply remember the original compliment," replied Annabell, wondering why she felt so at home with this man, feeling as if the sofa were an intimate, floating island surrounded by a feathered and bejewelled sea.

"Are you enjoying London?" asked Lord Varleigh, breaking the companionable silence. His hand was stretched along the back of the sofa, and Annabelle felt as excited and exhilarated as if he had put his arm round her shoulders.

"Oh, yes," she breathed, trying to fight against the realisation that she was enjoying herself completely for the first time. "I love all the parties and balls and operas. And I loved the City of London."

"When were you there?" asked her companion idly.

"Captain MacDonald took me for a drive some days ago," said Annabelle. "And then we went all round London. We even went as far as Highgate Village!"

"I shall be adventuring myself," said Lord Varleigh. "I am bound for Paris in the morning." The floating island bumped against the shores of hard reality. Paris and Lady Jane, thought Lord Varleigh, looking down at Annabelle's bent head. Now why did I let Jane cozen me into taking her along? Habit, I suppose. And I am

77

surely too old to start paying court to virgins like Miss Quennell.

"Paris!" exclaimed Annabelle in a small voice. "For how long, my lord?"

"For several months, I believe."

"Business affairs?"

"Pleasure."

"Oh."

Annabelle sat very still, suddenly intent on the pictures on her Chinese fan.

"With Lady Jane?" she said at last.

"With Lady Jane."

Never was Annabelle more glad to see the Captain than at that moment. "I hope you enjoy your journey, Lord Varleigh," said Annabelle and, turning away, laid her hand on the large Captain's arm and smiled up at him so brilliantly that several of the watchers were convinced the cancellation of the engagement had all been a hum.

Lord Varleigh watched them go. They were both young and very well suited he thought from the great height of his thirty-two years. He was fond of Annabelle, he told himself, and he was glad to see her enjoying her ball.

He suddenly felt very liverish and ill at ease. He would be better off at his club. Paris beckoned, and by the time he returned, Annabelle would probably be married.

DURING the month following Lord Varleigh's departure to Paris, Annabelle found herself more in Captain MacDonald's company than ever before.

They rode in the Ring in Hyde Park, they attended the Jubilee celebrations, and they danced and dined with society in that long hot summer of parties. The war was over, the French defeated, and the celebrations and fireworks went on as the troops from Bordeaux—except those lucky enough to be dispatched across the Atlantic to fight the Americans—were returning in the hundreds, hungry and wounded. They had been taken from the gutter and to the gutter they returned. They had done what the nation needed, and the nation didn't want them anymore.

The officers, such as the Captain, were lucky enough to return to the world of society and to go on as if they had never left it. Who wanted to hear of Salamanca when there were so many delicious court scandals to discuss?

Captain MacDonald was quiet and civil. There were no more drunken episodes, no more amorous overtures, and he made an easy, undemanding companion. Annabelle had not discovered any man to fall in love with but many who were prepared to fall in love with her and found the Captain an effective barrier to their pursuit. Little by little they drifted closer together during the long, lazy summer days, sharing small jokes that only they knew the meaning of, exploring London, attending parties and balls.

Lady Emmeline felt triumphant. The Captain was following her instructions to the letter, and Annabelle was falling neatly into the oldest trap of all—propinquity.

Lady Emmeline was admittedly disappointed that Annabelle had lost a certain zest, a certain spark of independence. She was unfailingly dutiful, pleasant and submissive and, to the old dowager's way of thinking, appeared to be in danger of becoming a bore.

Then Lady Emmeline fell ill with a high fever. The physician was called and failed to diagnose the cause of the illness, but he recommended that the Dowager Marchioness should be removed to more salubrious surroundings since even the elegant squares of the West

End were beginning to smell ripe under the heat of the summer sun.

Annabelle enlisted the aid of Countess Honeyford and rented an attractive villa. The villa proved to be a small palace in Kensington Gore, standing back behind a high wall. It had three acres of garden on the south side, and the large rooms ran the whole length of the house from north to south. There was a library, a long gallery, two studies, and a suite of entertaining rooms. It was the most charming house Annabelle had ever seen. The doors were panelled with mirrors, the sofas and chairs were covered with apple-green damask, the drawing room was crimson and gold, and the long gallery and the library were green. Peacocks strutted on the terrace during the day, and nightingales sang their serenades in the garden after dark.

Annabelle felt sure that her frivolous godmother would be delighted with her bedroom when she recovered from her illness and could see it. It was in blue and gold with blue damask hangings and a large Malmaison bed.

The library was Annabelle's favorite, a great sunlit room filled with the scent of woodsmoke, potpourri and calf bindings, brimming with buhl and ormolu, pier glass and statues as well as delightful sofa tables from Gillow's fashionable warehouse, Sèvres china, and singing clocks.

The house belonged to a shady relative of the Countess's who had fled to France after some scandal. Whatever the relative's wrongdoing, Annabelle had to admit that he had excellent taste.

Society did not journey out to Kensington to visit the old lady or her beautiful goddaughter, and even the Captain only left his floral tributes at the lodge house at the gate. It was feared Lady Emmeline's fever was contagious.

Annabelle found that she did not mind the long hours of nursing. Horley, the maid, was surprisingly helpful, burying her animosity towards the girl so long as her mistress needed help.

Day after day the Dowager Marchioness tossed and turned and rambled in her delirium, and each day the doctor came and prophesied the worst.

Annabelle had never been so alone in her life. The servants were so well trained they were almost invisible.

When Horley relieved her at the sickbed, she would escape to the calm of the library to sit dreaming over a book or to simply stare out at the peace and quiet of the garden. Although they were very near London, they could have been miles away. Annabelle prayed that some of the peace of their surroundings would penetrate to poor Lady Emmeline's fevered brain. She had stopped the physician from bleeding the old lady any further, fearing that Lady Emmeline would become too weak to battle the fever.

One evening she returned to the sickroom and found Horley kneeling beside the bed, the tears streaming down her sallow cheeks. "She's gone, miss," sobbed Horley. "Just like that!"

Annabelle crossed slowly to the great bed and stood looking down at the waxen figure. She had never seen death before but despite Lady Emmeline's graveyard pallor, felt sure she was not seeing it now. She seized a looking glass from the dressing table and held it before the Dowager Marchioness's mouth. Nothing.

And then the glass began to mist. Annabelle felt the old lady's brow. It was cool and damp.

She took a deep breath. "God be praised, Horley," she said. "My lady is not dead. The fever has abated and she sleeps."

Horley got briskly to her feet. Drying her tears with

the hem of her apron, she looked at Annabelle with all the old dislike. "Then I shall watch by her bedside until she wakes," she said briskly. "There will be no need for your services this night, Miss Annabelle." Then she bobbed a curtsy and added reluctantly, "Not that I'm not grateful for all your help."

Annabelle hesitated a minute beside the bedside. But Lady Emmeline did indeed seem to be in the depths of a refreshing sleep. She left Horley to her charge and returned to the library.

The tall figure of a man was standing over by the long windows looking out across the garden. He turned as she entered the room and made a magnificent leg.

Annabelle responded with a deep curtsy. "So you are returned from Paris, my Lord Varleigh," she said in a carefully calm social tone. "You have no doubt not yet heard that Lady Emmeline has been sick of the fever."

"I did," he replied simply, "and that is why I am here. Is she better? Has the fever abated?"

Annabelle told him her good news, trying to keep the surprise from her face. This was one member of society at least who did not seem to be worried about infection.

"Then that is good news," he said, smiling down at her in such a way that her heart gave a wrench. "Come and walk with me in the garden and tell me all the latest on-dits."

"I fear I am sadly out of touch," said Annabelle, moving out through the windows and onto the mossy terrace. "I would rather hear your news of Paris. Was it very exciting?"

"Depressing, rather," said Lord Varleigh, tucking her small hand in his arm. "It was like stepping back into the last century."

He went on to describe the dark streets, ankle-deep in mud and filled with grimacing, posturing blackguards.

She was filled with horror as he described the filthy theaters where even the rich spat on the floor and used their knives as toothpicks and were crammed to capacity, their Napoleonic inscriptions painted over with fleurs-de-lis.

Paris, said Lord Varleigh, showed no signs of being a conquered capital or the French of being a conquered race. On the night after the allies' entry, he was told that the theaters and public gardens were packed as if nothing had happened. The cynical French were impenitent at the suffering they had caused. There indifference to death remained the same. At Montmartre, where the Russians stormed their way into Paris over the bodies of the boys of the Military College, corpses were carefully preserved for sightseers, and houses pitted with bullets bore notices, "Ici on voit la bataille pour deux sous!" "Here one can see the battle for two sous!"

Despite his dislike of the worldy Parisians, Lord Varleigh said he could not help but be impressed by Napoleon's great public buildings. It was like another world, he told the fascinated Annabelle, to find all this order and splendor in the middle of a dark medieval jungle of twisted streets and filthy houses.

He praised the splendid prospect from the summit of the Elysian fields with the road descending through masses of trees to the Tuileries. Incredible!

"How I should love to see it all!" cried Annabelle, and then sensed a stiffness and reserve in her companion and wondered what she had said to upset him.

Lord Varleigh was thinking how Lady Jane had thrived in Paris among the indolent, pleasure-loving crowd. There were no gentlemen and certainly no ladies. Even Napoleon himself, now exiled on Elba, had observed, "They are all rascals." Her rapacious demands for money, for clothes and jewels, and gold for gambling, had increased. She had gained a great deal of weight from sampling all the gastronomic delights of Very's, Hardis, and the Quadron Bleu, even breakfasting greedily with intending duellists at Tortoni's off pâtés, game, fish, broiled kidneys, iced champagne and liqueurs.

He had finally told her the liaison was at an end, and a horrendous scene had followed. She had accused him of being in love with Annabelle Quennell. She had torn her hair like a madwoman and uttered threats against Annabelle's life. Never had he had to extract himself from an affair with such scenes of ranting and raving.

Now all he wanted to do was walk in the English garden in the failing light under the old cedars with this quiet girl on his arm and breath in the peace. He told himself he felt a fatherly affection for Annabelle and put down his feeling of well-being to being safely back home away from foreign scenes and foreign voices.

"It is time I settled down," he said quietly, and Annabelle's heart missed a beat. A nightingale sang from the bushes, a clear heartrending melody, and the sky dimmed from pale green to dark blue.

"I feel I have neglected my estates for too long," he went on, "and I am weary of the social round. But tell me about yourself," he added in a light voice. "I gather from the gossips that your engagement to Captain MacDonald is shortly to be renewed."

What a noisy bird that is, thought Annabelle, glaring at the unseen nightingale. "Perhaps I shall marry Captain MacDonald," she said defiantly. "He is good company."

"And is that all you feel for him?" persisted the now-mocking voice beside her. They had nearly reached the gates, and she turned and faced him. Her face seemed to swim below his in the evening light.

"My private life is my own affair, my lord," she said coldly.

He took her hands in his and drew her towards him, his eyes glinting strangely in the dim twilight. A twig snapped near them and both turned and stared towards the gates. A dark figure slid off into the night.

"Who's there?" called Lord Varleigh. He released Annabelle's hands and ran to the gates. No one.

"Strange," he murmured, returning to Annabelle. "Have any more strange things happened to Lady Emmeline while I have been away?"

Annabelle shook her head. "Not one. Godmother is convinced that she was the subject of some mad wager."

"Possibly," he said thoughtfully. "What do you think?"

Annabelle suddenly remembered Mad Meg's strange warning and shivered. "I think it must be as she says," she replied. "No one has tried to harm her since that party on Mr. Hullock's boat."

"And no one has tried to harm you either?" he teased. "No gentlemen kissing you over the champagne glasses?"

Annabelle glared at him like an angry kitten. "*No one* has had the *effrontery*, my lord."

"Strange," he said, "and you so kissable."

"As is Lady Jane," replied Annabelle, walking before him into the house.

"You are impertinent."

"One impertinence deserves another," said Annabelle tartly. "We are not chaperoned, my lord, so please leave the library door open."

"On the contrary," he said coldly, "I shall close it now—behind me when I leave. Servant, Miss Quennell."

He made a magnificent leg, turned on his heel, and departed.

Annabelle ran to the window to watch him leave and then stayed for a long time on the terrace, listening to the sound of his horse's hooves galloping off in the distance until she could hear them no more.

Chapter Eight

AFTER SEVERAL DAYS Horley pronounced her ladyship fully recovered, and the Dowager Marchioness was moved to a daybed in the drawing room.

But Annabelle found her more eccentric than ever. She lay around in toilettes that would have shocked a demimondaine and sometimes, when she thought no one was watching, flirted and ogled with the shadows in the corners of the long room, vividly conjuring up, with every ancient coquettish gesture, the ghosts of the eighteenth century: the bright brocade dresses of the ladies, the embroidered coats of the gentlemen; the men with their faces polished and the ladies with theirs painted. The ladies wore their hair piled up over their heads, augmented with pads and the whole greased with pomatum and dusted with powder. The elaborate play of the gilded figures, scented handkerchiefs, simpering and giggling; gross brutality mixed with refinement.

The scent of musk and unwashed flesh floated round Lady Emmeline in a large yellow cloud. Annabelle's tactful suggestion that Lady Emmeline would feel better after a bath was met with horror and upraised hands. All windows were tightly shut, and the early autumn evening blazed with color on the other side of the glass like some exquisite, unattainable picture.

Captain MacDonald had erupted onto the scene again, walking with Annabelle in the gardens or even sitting reading to Lady Emmeline. The latter was a heavy task for both reader and listener as every sentence of the story seemed to remind the Captain of something old so-and-so had said the other day, and off he would go into a long digression.

When the Captain was nervous or slightly bosky, there was a reckless strung-up quality to him which was very attractive, but when he was relaxed as he seemed to be these days, Annabelle had to confess that she found him a bore.

Before her godmother's illness Annabelle had been gently drifting into marriage with the Captain. Now she seemed to be drifting gently away.

One day at the end of September Lady Emmeline finally decided herself well enough to hold a party. Cards were sent out, the windows were at last flung open, and all the rooms were aired. Society flowed out from London, for the Dowager Marchioness was noted for her French chef and her lavish hospitality.

Annabelle, Lady Emmeline, and the Captain received the guests, and Annabelle noticed with a twinge of dismay that she was quite clearly marked down as being the Captain's property.

Then—quite suddenly—before she had time to control her expression, Lord Varleigh strolled elegantly into the room. His face looked very tanned against the dazzling white of his intricate cravat. Annabelle looked across the room at him with her heart in her eyes, but fortunately he had bent his head to say something to Lady Emmeline. By the time he looked in her direction, she had had time to control her feelings and pin a social smile on her face.

Several of the ladies were wearing becoming gowns designed by Annabelle. There was one particular design that Annabelle had put her heart and soul into—a confection of pale green Indian muslin trimmed with lily of the valley in a deep garland around the hem—and with a sinking heart she saw it was beautifying none other than Lady Jane Cherle.

Admittedly Varleigh's mistress had put on a great deal of weight but her skin was still magnificent, and her lazy, languid air of sensuality drew all the men to her like bees to a honey pot. Even Lord Varleigh fetched her refreshment while she dazzled and sparkled at him with the full force of her personality. In this, Lord Varleigh, that expert of the delicate affair, that tightrope walker of the circus of intrigue, made a dangerous error: The row in Paris had become a lover's quarrel in Jane's ever-optimistic mind.

Annabelle fell prey to the most terrible pangs of jealousy. She could not help noticing that when Lord Varleigh paused beside her to ask her quietly how she was, Lady Jane did not even seem to mind. Now the evening might have continued quietly had not Annabelle been a very human girl.

Lord Varleigh was complimenting Annabelle on her appearance with his usual expertise, and she smiled dazzlingly up at him and then, on impulse, flashed a triumphant look across the room full into the eyes of her rival. With feminine satisfaction Annabelle watched Lady Jane's thin-pencilled brows snap together.

"It is a trifle warm, my lord," said Annabelle.

She looked in the direction of the terrace, and he smiled down at her in a way that did something peculiar to her heart. Taking her small gloved hand in his own, he said lightly, "Then shall we promenade outside? You can tell me whether you and the Captain have been taking any more interesting drives."

Annabelle did not want to talk about the Captain, but as they walked out onto the terrace, she became aware of Lady Jane's efforts to catch their attention, and moved closer to Lord Varleigh, smiling up at him in a bewitching way from under her long lashes.

There was a sound of breaking glass from the room behind them as Lady Jane's glass fell from her trembling fingers.

She erupted onto the terrace in a flurry of silks and confronted the pair while the society that filled the rooms behind stopped talking and turned to view the drama with avid interest. There hadn't been a really good scandal in *weeks*.

"Has he mounted you yet?" she demanded of Annabelle, her magnificent eyes flashing with fury.

"No," replied Annabelle and with what she hoped was the gentle answer which turneth away wrath, "I do not horse ride."

"I'm talking about another kind of beast—the one with two backs," shrilled Lady Jane while the watching guests gasped and exclaimed in fits of delicious horror.

Annabelle's puzzled, innocent stare would have driven Lady Jane to further vulgarity, but to the audience's immense disappointment, just as Lady Jane was opening her mouth wide to let fly the next salvo, Lord Varleigh stuffed his lace handkerchief into it and, clipping the infuriated Lady Jane's arms behind her back, marched her off into the shrubbery.

Her cheeks pink with mortification, Annabelle turned with relief to the ever-present Captain and accepted his offer of refreshment. Lady Jane was not seen again that evening, but Lord Varleigh rejoined the party much later. Tables and chairs had been pushed aside as the guests clamored for waltzes. The musicians struck up a lively air, and Annabelle found herself being swept into the steps of the waltz while the Captain, who had been about to ask her himself, looked on with a baffled air.

"I am sorry you were subjected to such a vulgar

scene," said Lord Varleigh, looking down at Annabelle's embarrassed face.

"Your affairs are no concern of mine, my lord," said Annabelle quietly.

"Lady Jane has made our late affair your concern. I am sorry for it," he said simply. "Come, smile at me, Miss Quennell, and let us be friends."

Annabelle gave him a reluctant smile and then realised he had referred to his *late* affair. Her smile grew wider and her little feet seemed to float across the floor.

Captain MacDonald leaned against a pillar and watched them, one large finger playing with his luxuriant side-whiskers. He did not like the uncharacteristic warmth in Varleigh's eyes any more than he liked the high color on Annabelle's cheek or her shining eyes.

Something would have to be done—and quickly!

THE following day was warm and misty although the leaves were beginning to change color to red and gold, and the fruit hung heavy in the apple trees in the orchard.

The Captain appeared in a smart phaeton and pair and cunningly solicited Lady Emmeline's permission to take Annabelle for a drive before asking that young lady herself. Annabelle was strangely reluctant to go, but Lady Emmeline's pleasure at seeing her once more in the company of Captain MacDonald was obvious, and Annabelle did not have the heart to disappoint the old lady.

Annabelle exclaimed in surprise at the trunks corded up behind the phaeton, and the Captain explained he was to visit the mother of one of his fallen comrades in Chiswick and perform the melancholy duty of handing over her son's effects.

Annabelle wondered why she felt nervous. She was, after all, used to driving out with the Captain. Perhaps it was because he seemed to be secretly excited about something. The mist coiled through the trees at the edge of Kensington High Road, turning pale yellow as a tiny sun appeared very far above.

When they stopped at a toll gate, Annabelle had an impulse to ask the Captain to turn back. Then she put her fears down to the strangeness of the weather. The lamps on the toll gate were still lit and shone through the coiling mist. An old and torn recruiting poster flapped against the wall of the toll in a sudden puff of wind. It was urging new recruits to repair "to Mr. Bigg's Hibernian, jovial, overflowing punch bowl, North-side, Old Dock: where an officer waits with *impatience* and *British guineas* to receive those heroes that are emulous of *glory*. God save great George our King. Huzza! Damn the French!"

Well, the great King George was now mad and raving, locked behind the walls of his palace while the Prince Regent enjoyed the British public's contempt.

The phaeton jerked forward, and Annabelle let down her veil as the dust began to swirl around them as the Captain sprang his horses.

The countryside seemed to flash past at a great rate. The sun rose higher, burning away the mist, and the fields spread out on either side under a pale blue sky.

Annabelle forgot her fears and settled back to enjoy the scenery. They flew past the Bath stagecoach which did the London-to-Bath journey in "three days if God permits." Annabelle was glad that she had never had to endure a journey by stagecoach. On fine days such as this it looked splendid, bowling along with a spanking team with the tootling of the guard on his yard-long horn. But in bad weather Annabelle knew that the passengers inside almost died of the smell while the passengers outside often died of exposure. Coaches often lost the road or capsized or sank into it, and a fine day like today was not even free from peril. If the coachman drove too fast, there was danger of fire, for the wheels created a perilous friction on the axles.

Soon they had slowed to a trot and were proceeding decorously along Chiswick Mall. The Captain swung off the Mall and then through a bewildering network of small roads, finally coming to a stop outside a pair of fine wrought-iron gates.

An evil-looking gatekeeper came limping out in answer to their summons.

"Fine day, Cap'n" he said, tugging his forelock. "Missus ain't home and sarvents is out, but missus says her'll be back drecktly and youse is to make yesselfs comfortable."

The Captain threw the man a piece of gold, and the gatekeeper caught it as deftly as a monkey and bit it with the stumps of his blackened teeth.

They moved slowly up a pitted and unkempt driveway past mossy statues, obviously relics of some ancestor's Grand Tour. The house was Palladian with a great central dome and porticoed entrance.

It was all very dismal, reflected Annabelle, and somehow sinister, wrapped in its atmosphere of autumnal decay. I am becoming too fanciful, she thought and allowed the Captain to escort her into the house.

He led the way into a drawing room on the ground floor, and then, muttering something about having to have a word with the gatekeeper, he left Annabelle alone.

The room smelled musty and damp, and the faded pink and green of its walls showed great stains of damp moisture near the ceiling. Someone had been recently and inexpertly dusting, for great cobwebs still hung from the cornices and there was at least half an inch of dust under the silent clock on the mantelshelf. A tarnished silver tray rested on a low table containing decanters and a plate of biscuits. There was no other sign that they were expected or even that the house was inhabited.

There came a furtive scurrying sound from behind the walls.

Rats.

Annabelle began to feel cold despite the day outside. She wondered if the house was haunted by the dead soldier's ghost. Out in the garden the statues bordering the drive stared back at her with their blind stone eyes. The day was very still and quiet apart from the sinister rustling in the wainscoating.

There was no sign of the Captain returning, and Annabelle began to feel increasingly uneasy. She decided to search the house and see if she could find some servant who might tell her where the lady of the house was. One by one she pushed open the doors of the downstairs rooms and stood and stared in amazement. They were thick with dust, their furniture shrouded under holland covers. In a green saloon the dust stretched in an unbroken gray sea on the uncarpeted floor.

A cold hand of fear clutched at her stomach. She walked slowly upstairs and pushed open door after door; at last she found one room prepared and ready. It was a vast bedroom which had been recently swept and cleaned by an inexpert hand. A fire was made up on the hearth, and clean sheets had been put on the bed. Annabelle breathed a sigh of relief. The lady of the house had obviously fallen on hard times and could only afford to live in two rooms and probably only had one or two servants.

Feeling more cheerful, she returned to the drawing room where the Captain was toasting his boots in front of the fire.

"No sign of anyone yet," he said cheerfully. "Have some wine, Annabelle, and relax. Her name's Mrs.

Creedy, and the gatekeeper said she should not be too long."

They sat for a long time, watching the statues' shadows lengthening on the uncut lawns and talking in a desultory fashion.

The sun went down in a blaze of gold and crimson, and the mist uncoiled itself from the dew-soaked lawns, and still Mrs. Creedy did not return.

LORD Varleigh had called in at White's in St. James's Street. The harvests were in on his estates. He had assisted the farmers—hence his healthy tan—and now felt he owed himself an evening's relaxation.

But for him the glamour of the famous club had gone. Beau Brummell and his cronies held court at the recently constructed bow window overlooking the street. Bloods and bucks, Corinthians and Dandies crouched over the gambling tables, and an almost religious silence prevailed.

He wished he had not come to Town and wondered if he should forego an evening of cards for the calm pleasure of a visit to Kensington Gore. What an incalculable, impertinent girl was Annabelle Quennell! At times he was not even sure that he liked her. But he would go after all. The girl was never boring and one never knew what she might say.

With a sinking heart he saw the club bore, Mr. Garforth, edging towards him. He rose to leave, but it was too late.

"Thought you knew all the gossip in town," said Mr. Garforth petulantly, by way of an opening.

"What don't I know?" asked Lord Varleigh, resigning himself.

"Didn't know the Creedys were in residence?" said Mr. Garforth. "In fact, after old Creedy's cheating at cards and unpaid debts over half of London, I never thought he would dare to show his face this side of the Channel again."

"He obviously has," yawned Lord Varleigh, "if that is what you are trying to tell me."

"Well, I didn't *see* the Creedy fellow," said Mr. Garforth, "but they're receiving callers. Drove past Chiswick—you know that deserted barn of a place they've got—and who should I see driving in to call but Captain Jimmy MacDonald and that girl, Miss Quennell. Know her, don't you? Well, you might drop a word in her ear that it ain't quite the thing to know the Creedys. Surprised at Jimmy MacDonald. He's wild, that one, but he's up to snuff when it comes to who one ought to know and who one oughtn't."

Lord Varleigh sat very still. "Are you sure the Creedys are back in residence?" he asked. "I saw them in Paris surrounded by a lot of fellow wastrels a month ago."

"Stands to reason they must be," said Mr. Garforth, pleased with the rare interest he was eliciting. "People don't go calling on empty houses. I say, I haven't finished yet."

But Lord Varleigh had gone.

ALL Annabelle's nervousness had returned. The Captain had nearly finished the contents of the decanters and resolutely and stubbornly turned aside all suggestions they should leave.

Annabelle at last came to a decision.

"I cannot remain under this roof with you for much longer, sir," she said severely. "I feel I am being sadly compromised as it is."

The Captain surveyed her from heavy-lidded eyes. "What a stubborn girl you are," he remarked. "We ain't going anywhere, so make up your mind to that."

"What!" cried Annabelle, outraged. "Take me home this instant, sir!"

"No," said the Captain, refilling his glass.

Annabelle got to her feet. "Then I shall have to walk," she said, resolutely turning towards the door.

A large hand pulled her back. "Unhand me, sir!" cried Annabelle while a corner of her brain marvelled that she had actually used those words, so beloved of fairy-tale heroines.

The Captain pushed her into a chair. "Don't ask me to use force," he said quietly, and Annabelle realised with a start of surprise that he was not drunk at all although his eyes glittered strangely.

"I have no taste for rape," went on the Captain calmly as if he were discussing some new dish. "But yes, my dear, you are going to be compromised. I am going to keep you here for as long as it takes London to find we have gone off together. That prime bore, Garforth, saw us entering here and saw you going with me willingly."

"But Mrs. Creedy . . ." began Annabelle.

"Mrs. Creedy," interrupted the Captain with great good humor, "is, I believe, in Paris with her card-sharping husband."

"And the son?"

"Haven't got one. Those trunks are full of any clothes we may find necessary, although if you behave like a sensible girl, we should not find clothes necessary at all."

Annabelle went as red as a beetroot. A vivid picture of the cleaned and prepared bedroom upstairs sprang into her mind. And even if she should escape the Captain, the gatekeeper must be in his pay and would stop her before she reached the road.

"How could you *bear* to be married to someone who has to be *forced* to go to the altar with you?"

"Easily," said Captain MacDonald, getting to his feet. "If she's as pretty as you."

He jerked her out of the chair and pulled her to him and forced his mouth down on hers. Annabelle felt her senses reeling from lack of oxygen rather than passion.

To the Captain's surprise she went limp in his arms and, feeling that the battle was won, he relaxed his hold before bending to her mouth again.

She leaned round him, and her fingers groped for the Captain's snuffbox. With a dexterity which would have drawn praise from Petersham himself, she flicked up the enameled lid and then freed her mouth from the Captain's embrace.

"Darling," she said huskily.

The Captain drew back and looked down at her in surprise and triumph.

She whipped round the snuffbox and threw the entire contents straight into his face. While the Captain clawed his face and coughed and spluttered, Annabelle picked up one of the decanters and, closing her eyes tightly, brought it down with a *crrump* on the Captain's head. He sank to the floor and lay motionless.

With trembling fingers Annabelle felt for his pulse but, as always happens on these nerveracking occasions, could feel or hear nothing but the tumultuous beating of her heart. She drew a small steel mirror from her reticule and tried to keep her hands from shaking as she held it over his mouth, bringing a sharp memory of doing the same thing to her godmother. The glass misted, and the Captain let out a stentorian snore.

Annabelle fled out into the grounds and stood irresolute. A loud voice hailing the gatekeeper made her nearly jump from her skin. Friend or enemy? Probably enemy.

She looked wildly round for a place to hide, and then as she heard the sound of shouts and blows from the gatehouse, plunged headlong into the tangled shrubbery and lay still.

Carriage wheels rattled up the drive and swept past her hiding place, but Annabelle was too frightened to look out.

Resplendent in a many-caped driving coat and with his long riding whip clutched in his hand, Lord Varleigh sprang lightly down from his carriage and, tilting back his curly brimmed beaver, stared up at the house which seemed to stare back at him with a sad and deserted air. Then he noticed a light burning in one of the downstairs windows.

With an oath he strode into the dark hallway and with a great crash swung open the double doors of the drawing room.

One look at the villainous gatekeeper had been enough to convince Lord Sylvester Varleigh that Captain MacDonald was up to no good. The wretched little man had tried to bar his entry and had gone down under Lord Varleigh's punishing left. What he expected to find, he did not know, but the last thing he expected was the scene that met his eyes.

Of Annabelle there was not the slightest sign. But Captain MacDonald was sitting up in the middle of a large pool of Burgundy, nursing his head and groaning.

Lord Varleigh seized him by the lapels and dragged him to his feet. "Where is she?" he demanded, giving the groaning Captain a shake.

"Gone," moaned the Captain. "Hell cat! Threw snuff in my face and crashed me on the head with the Burgundy decanter. Gone!"

"What did you do it for? Why?" said Lord Varleigh, shaking him again.

"Don't do that!" said the large Captain crossly, jerking

himself free. "I'm in love with her, that's why."

"It's a funny way of showing love," said Lord Varleigh. "You must have terrified her out of her wits."

"What do you know of love?" said the Captain, slumping down in an armchair and holding his aching head in his hands. "Don't like to get personal, Varleigh, but all you know is what you pay for. I'm crazy out of my head with love for Annabelle. She's everything a woman should be—feminine and kind and good—except," he added wryly, "when she's hitting me on the head."

Lord Varleigh looked at him in silence, two spots of color burning on his thin cheeks under his tan. The Captain's remarks had struck home—"all you know is what you pay for." He compared Lady Jane's vulgar, sensuous, rapacious greed with Annabelle's delicate virginity and was overcome with a wave of fear for her welfare.

"We must not stay here bandying words," said Lord Varleigh. "She may be wandering through Chiswick, and God knows what evils could happen to her this time of night."

"You're right, egad!" cried the Captain, staggering to his feet. The room swung round, and he sank back in his chair again with a groan. "You'll need to go, Varleigh," he said. "But I put you on your honor as a gentleman. Swear you will present my case to Miss Quennell fairly. Tell her I did it because I love her. Swear!"

"You have my word," said Lord Varleigh quietly. "If I should not return, you will know that I have found her."

He swung himself into his carriage outside the Creedy mansion. Frost was rimming the grass, glittering like diamonds under the pale light of a thin, new moon. He was about to set off when his eye was caught by what seemed to be a scrap of material lying under the shrubbery.

He got down and walked towards the bushes. There was a flash of white and the material disappeared. Must be a rabbit, he thought and was about to turn away when his sharp ear caught the faint sounds of quick, frightened breathing. He pushed back the bushes and bent down. The chalk-white, tearstained face of Annabelle Quennell stared up at him.

"Come out," he said gently. "It's all over now. I will take you home."

He helped Annabelle to her feet. She was shivering with cold, and her thin muslin dress was plastered to her body in a way that would have delighted the eye of her rakish godmother.

"Let us go in first and tell Captain MacDonald you are safe."

"No!" squeaked Annabelle. "I won't. I won't go back there!"

"Very well," said Lord Varleigh. "I shall go myself and tell Captain . . ."

"No!" cried Annabelle again, clutching his arm. "Don't go! Please don't leave me. Take me away from here!"

Lord Varleigh saw that she was nearly hysterical. Best to get her away.

He helped her up into the carriage, wrapped her tenderly in a large bearskin rug, and apologised for the fact that she had to travel in a high-perched phaeton on such a cold evening.

"Oh, cease the gallantries," snapped the ungrateful Miss Quennell. "I don't care if I have to go home in a *wheelbarrow*."

Lord Varleigh looked at her in some amusement. She had lost her bonnet in the bushes, and her masses of red-gold hair were cascading down on her shoulders. As she sat huddled in the bearskin, she looked to Lord Varleigh like a cavewoman whose husband has just failed to kill a saber-toothed tiger for the cooking pot. He told her so and received a small snort of disgust in reply.

After several attempts to engage his companion in conversation, Lord Varleigh gave up the effort and sprang his horses instead, leaving Chiswick behind in a cloud of dust.

When he turned in at the villa in Kensington Gore, it was to find the house in darkness. No worried Lady Emmeline was waiting up. Horley, roused from her slumbers, said acidly that her ladyship had to watch her health and not sit up waiting for inconsiderate folk to come home with the milk. She got severely reprimanded by Lord Varleigh for her insolence.

A sleepy footman lighted the fire in the library and produced a tray of tea things. Lord Varleigh had stated he had something of importance to say to Miss Annabelle Quennell on the matter of love, and Miss Quennell found herself suddenly wide awake and rather breathless.

Annabelle, still wrapped in the bearskin rug, warmed her damp slippers by the fire and turned a glowing face up to Lord Varleigh. He leaned his arm along the mantelshelf and looked down at her thoughtfully.

"My dear Miss Quennell," he said, suddenly feeling very old and pompous, "it is sometimes hard to recognise real love. So much nonsense is talked about love and so much nonsense is written about it that it is sometimes hard to recognise the real thing."

But I recognise it, thought Annabelle with a start of surprise. She watched his handsome, high-nosed face as he looked down into the blazing fire. I'm in love with him, she thought. I've been in love with him since that dreadful night at the opera.

"Now, the Captain is really very much in love with you," said Lord Varleigh. "I would have punished him for his mad behavior today otherwise."

He stopped and looked down in surprise at Annabelle. One minute her face had been glowing and tender and the next it was almost contorted with fury.

"Captain MacDonald . . . loves *me*. Don't be so naïve, my lord. The Captain wishes to force me into marriage because my godmother has promised him money an' he marries me. And you *drivel* on about love. You know nothing of the matter yourself, sirrah!"

It was the second time that evening that Lord Varleigh had been accused of knowing nothing of love, and he was beginning to become irritated.

"I am convinced the Captain's motives were not mercenary," he said stiffly.

"If you are in love with someone," said Annabelle with a maddening air of weary patience, "then you neither frighten them or hurt them. I am tired of sitting here talking nonsense, my lord, and I wish to go to bed."

He gave her a cold bow and walked towards the door.

Moved by a sudden impulse, Annabelle called after him. "Forgive me, my lord. I did not mean to sound so harsh. I am shaken and upset. I have endured the most horrible evening of my life. I am in no mood to hear of love from anyone." *Except you*, muttered a treacherous voice in her brain.

He smiled at her and came back and took her small hand in his long fingers and turning it over pressed a light kiss on the palm.

"I understand and accept your apology, Annabelle

Quennell," he said lightly and bowed his way out.

Annabelle sat for a long time with the hand he had kissed clenched, curled up into a fist. She felt very, very homesick for the rectory and for her father's kind face.

Chapter Nine

LORD SYLVESTER VARLEIGH could now persuade himself that he had thoroughly attended to his duties as a landlord. Since the evening of Annabelle's rescue, he had retired to his estates and had overseen extensive repairs to his house, his farms, and his tenants' cottages. Now, he had to admit to himself, he was frankly bored with his own company.

His boots left a line of black footprints across the frost-rimed grass. A red sun was shining low on the horizon. Piles of hay put down for the deer lay about under the trees of the park, and blackbirds crossed and crisscrossed the frosty grass in their search for worms, leaving long lines of black arrows.

His home, Varleigh Court, was spread out behind him with its square turrets and gray walls, and the thin lines of smoke from its many chimneys rose straight into the metallic blue of the early morning sky.

He had to remind himself he had not been completely alone. There had been some good hunting days and duty calls on the local county. But he had known them all since he was a boy, and he now wondered why he should feel so alone and set apart from their well-ordered lives and families.

He suddenly stopped. That was it. Families!

All the country houses he had visited had echoed with the yells and cries of children, and the rooms had been filled with groups of relatives from close cousins to aunts twice removed.

He, himself, had few relatives, and most of them were elderly and lived far away in other counties.

Lord Varleigh was suddenly beset with that malaise which attacks even the most sophisticated Englishman in his prime—the sudden and awful desire to get married. Not to anyone in particular, but to some well-bred faceless girl who would fill his nursery with healthy sons.

He would give a house party, he decided, and invite at least three suitable girls. He turned abruptly and walked back to the Court. Cards must be sent out and bedrooms aired. He sent for the housekeeper, butler, and groom of the chambers and issued rapid instructions as if he were preparing for a military campaign. And flowers. He must have flowers. In all the rooms.

His ancient housekeeper, Mrs. Meany, shook her head afterwards and confided to the butler that my lord showed all the signs of a man about to be leg-shackled. "They always asks for flowers," she said, "and then 'fore you know it, you're preparing the wedding breakfast."

He then went into his study and started to compose a list of names. The guest list must be carefully worked out so that the girls he planned to look over would not guess they had been invited for that purpose. He would invite Lady Amelia Bunbury, a dashing redhead of impeccable lineage, along with her parents. Then there was pretty little Mrs. O'Harold, an entrancing widow, and the Honorable Caroline Dempsey, a buxom blonde with rather protruding teeth. An excellent horsewoman, she in fact looked rather like a horse. He went on scribbling busily while the frost melted from the grass and the red sun changed to gold.

Annabelle Quennell? Why not? And the Captain, of course. Captain MacDonald would see that he had kept his word and was doing his best to further the course of true love. And that old wretch, Lady Emmeline. He began to look forward to his house party immensely. He would propose to the lucky girl, get married after a decent interval, and then after another decent interval would have a noisy, healthy son to scamper along the stately corridors and bring some life to the old house.

"AN invitation to Varleigh Court," cried Lady Emmeline. "Marvellous. We shall go of course."

"Yes, Emmeline," said Annabelle, bending over her sewing to hide the look of pleasure on her face.

"I am bored with rusticating here," went on Lady Emmeline, "and Varleigh Court is vastly comfortable. He has invited Captain MacDonald as well, he says. How kind!"

How could he? thought Annabelle bitterly. After that night of fear and violence at Chiswick, she could hardly bear to look at the Captain. Lady Emmeline had dismissed the whole episode. It was, she said, exactly what she would have expected a red-blooded man like the Captain to do. As it was, Varleigh's meddling interference had saved Annabelle's virtue, so now they could all be comfortable again.

Annabelle tried to be pleasant to the Captain to please her eccentric godmother. She had hopefully expected the doors of the villa at Kensington Gore to be barred to him after his behavior at Chiswick. But Lady Emmeline seemed more pleased to see him than ever.

Lady Emmeline had grown increasingly eccentric. She had taken to wearing fur eyebrows and only seemed to remember to put one on at a time so that it looked as if she were carrying a hairy caterpillar around on her forehead. She had taken to wearing patches and a powdered wig to remind her of her youth, and she often talked and chatted to long-dead acquaintances with such vivacity that Annabelle feared for her reason.

Distressed by the Captain's frequent visits, worried and embarrassed by her godmother's eccentricity, and saddened because she no longer saw Lord Varleigh, Annabelle had written to her mother, begging to be allowed to return home, but her plea had only promoted a long letter from Mrs. Quennell. The rector's wife exclaimed over Annabelle's ingratitude and reminded her eldest daughter that it was her Christian duty to marry well and provide her younger sisters with husbands.

A visit to Lord Varleigh's home would be exciting, if only in a painful way. At least I shall see him, thought Annabelle and then chided herself for loving a man who showed only an avuncular interest in her at the very most.

Madame Croke had paid Annabelle generously for her designs, and Annabelle had hoarded the money carefully in case the strangeness of her present surroundings should one day prove too much for her. Surely her *own mother* would not turn her away if she arrived on the doorstep of the rectory.

Annabelle could not help dreaming of Sylvester Varleigh. His high-nosed aristocratic face had replaced the square, tanned face of her dream lover. She had never daydreamed much before, but now she found herself imagining all sorts of delightful adventures which would end in Lord Varleigh leading her to the altar. But apart from the presence of Lady Jane Cherle, there was her forceful and pushing mother to consider. The proud Lord Varleigh would surely not ally himself with any girl with such a mother.

She assured herself it was harmless to dream of him— an innocent pastime, no more. At times she could almost convince herself that she had forgotten what he looked like.

It had never entered Annabelle's dreams that when she arrived at Varleigh Court, there would be other *young* ladies present.

It was therefore with a feeling that she wryly identified as pique that she found herself in the company of three very young, attractive ladies on her first day at Varleigh Court.

Despite Lord Varleigh's precautions and the presence of many other guests and many small children, the three young ladies had quickly realised that they were "on trial" and discussed their prospects with Annabelle almost before she had had time to remove her hat. Several of the young gentlemen had already made a book, and the odds were in favor of Lady Amelia Bunbury with Mrs. O'Harold running a close second. To her chagrin Annabelle was considered "spoken for," and the three ladies eagerly demanded her advice on the best way to entrap their elegant host.

Annabelle had at last the young female companionship for which she had craved but not at all in the way she had wanted. Lady Jane was not present and that should have at least been a blessing, but on the contrary it depressed Annabelle immeasurably. She was disappointed in Lord Varleigh. By the time her trunks were unpacked, she had convinced herself that she did not love him one bit. He was no better than the rest of them. Marriage, in his mind, was obviously a business proposition.

In the following days the rather tedious life-style of an English country house in winter took over. The gentlemen went out shooting or hunted while the ladies gossiped, practised attitudes, netted purses, read, and yawned. Only in the evenings did the great house come to life after a long and elaborate dinner when childish games like Hunt the Slipper or Blind Man's Bluff were played, followed often by some dangerous romp which degenerated into cushion throwing and wild chases through the formal suite of entertaining rooms on the first floor. Mrs. O'Harold was nigh suffocated with a cushion held over her face by the dashing Lady Amelia and the pretty little Irish widow had struggled to her feet and retaliated by emptying the contents of a fruit bowl over that young lady's head.

Captain MacDonald showed an alarming tendency to become increasingly boisterous. The men hailed him as a capital gun and the ladies smiled and simpered and congratulated Annabelle on having secured such a flower of English manhood for a suitor.

Annabelle was hardly allowed to exchange more than two words with her host. He had only to enter the roc and he was immediately besieged by three young ladies and their hopeful parents. Annabelle contented herself with watching him from afar and deciding that she did not like him one little bit. She was quite sure that most of the time Lord Varleigh was not aware she was in the house.

She would have been very surprised to know just how mistaken she was. Lord Varleigh was heartily wishing he had never invited Annabelle Quennell. How could he possibly decide which lady would suit him best when Annabelle was glowing with beauty on the other side of the room? Returning from a long day's hunting, the Captain had spoken to Lord Varleigh at length of his undying passion for Annabelle and his hopes of marriage. Lord Varleigh had been moved to utter a few words of caution. Annabelle Quennell could not be *forced* into marriage. The Captain had hurriedly agreed but before he had turned his face away from Lord Varleigh to look across the barren wintry fields, Lord Varleigh had noticed a strangely childish, sulky, and stubborn look on the Captain's handsome face.

ANNABELLE had been used to rising very early in the morning in Yorkshire and she still found it impossible to lie late in bed. It was a relief to rise and get dressed and escape from the house for a solitary promenade in the icy gardens, made more formal looking by the steely grip of winter.

Her walks often took her as far as the pimping shed where an old Yorkshireman, Heckley, cut the faggots for the many fires of Varleigh Court. The pimping shed was comfortably redolent of all the woody smells of pine and birch and apple, and it was comforting to Annabelle to sit there listening to Heckley's homey burr and the crisp thwack of sharp ax on wood.

As she left Heckley one morning to return to the Court and join the others for breakfast, she reflected ruefully that she felt more at home with this old Yorkshire servant than with any of her fellow guests. With a little sigh she pushed open the door of the breakfast room . . . and stood still in dismay. Very few of the guests were there, but seated triumphantly at the head of the table, spearing grilled kidneys with great relish, was Lady Jane Cherle.

Was it not odd, she was telling her small audience, that her carriage pole should snap just outside the gates? But Sylvester would be *delighted* to see her.

Sylvester Varleigh, who entered the room some few minutes later, did not seem in the least ecstatic. His well-bred face was like a mask as he listened to Jane's voluble explanations. Lady Amelia, Mrs. O'Harold, and the Honorable Caroline Dempsey bristled like so many well-groomed cats.

Caroline was the first to move into the attack. "It seems too *convenient* of your carriage pole to break precisely outside my lord's gates, dear Lady Jane," she said with an awful smile. "In my case I should be at a loss to know what to do. *So* imposing to arrive uninvited, but then I am positively *hidebound* by the conventions. So silly, don't you think?"

"Yes," said Lady Jane with great unconcern.

Mrs. O'Harold gave tongue. "Well, I am sure that the repairs can be quickly finished and you can soon be on your way, Lady Jane. Where are you bound for?"

"Oh, someplace," yawned Jane. "It's beginning to snow, and Sylvester wouldn't turn his little Jane out on a day like this."

"Don't see why not," boomed Lady Amelia with a hearty laugh. "He puts the cats out at night. Joke," she added in unconvincing tones.

"He does!" said Lady Jane sweetly, raising her pencilled eyebrows in surprise. "And did you three ladies find it uncommonly cold out there?"

Annabelle giggled and Lady Jane's magnificent eyes rounded on her like two carriage lamps turning a sharp corner.

"Ah, little Miss Quennell. And when are you and the Captain to tie the knot? So *coy* to break off your engagement and then appear holding hands on every occasion."

"I do not hold hands with Captain MacDonald or anyone else for that matter," said Annabelle stiffly. "You must forgive me an' I sound harsh, Lady Jane, but I am not used to discussing my private life at the breakfast table."

"Little puss," said Lady Jane, giving Annabelle's cheek a painful pinch. "Then we shall have a lovely coze about it all at dinner. Can you find someone to show me my rooms, Sylvester dear?"

Lord Varleigh felt like wringing Lady Jane's neck, but he did not wish to perpetrate a scene in front of the other guests. He bowed his head and rang for the housekeeper.

Lady Jane rose, picked up a long fur boa, and slung it around her neck. The end of it, unfortunately, was trimmed with the paws and claws of several small animals, and it caught the Honorable Caroline full in the mouth.

"You did that on purpose," gasped Caroline, mottled with rage.

" 'Course I didn't, you silly goose," drawled Jane with a patronising laugh. "It's those teeth of yours, dear girl. They do stick out so. But I can recommend a very good dentist . . ."

She trailed out of the room in the wake of the housekeeper, leaving a fulminating silence behind. Lord Varleigh excused himself. Jane must go if he had to drag her through the gates.

"*Well!*" exclaimed Caroline, and the three rivals bent their heads together for the delicious task of rending Lady Jane's character and morals to shreds.

Annabelle suddenly felt she could not bear another

112

minute of it. The arrival of Lady Emmeline in scarlet and white striped morning dress and grotesque fur eyebrows proved to be the breaking point.

She muttered some excuse and fled to her rooms to fetch her bonnet and cloak. From along the corridor Lady Jane Cherle's voice rose and fell but the words were mercifully indistinguishable.

Annabelle escaped into the grounds and then stood irresolute. She decided to return to the pimping shed, to sit peacefully among the logs and listen to Heckley's soft Yorkshire voice which reminded her so painfully of home. She thought increasingly these days of the rectory, distance lending it an enchantment it did not possess. She had almost decided to send her savings home, but a nagging feeling of insecurity made her hold on to them. She had no idea what the journey north would cost but felt sure it would be a great deal.

She had written a long letter to her father, telling him of her earnings and begging him to say nothing until she came to a decision. The rector had sent a kind reply. The money was Annabelle's to spend as she wished. Her small savings would make little material difference to them. He could only beg her to be happy. Annabelle had not mentioned Lord Varleigh in her letter. Her gentle father would be shocked, she knew, to learn that his daughter had been hankering after an aristocrat whose morals—by rectory standards—were doubtful to say the least.

Heckley was not in the shed. Bundles of faggots, neatly tied with string, bore witness to his early morning's work. A stack of pine logs piled up in one corner exuded a pleasant aromatic smell.

Annabelle sat down gratefully on the pile of logs, enjoying the peace and quiet of the little shed. She began to feel sleepy after her earlier exertions and the emotional upheaval of the breakfast room. Her head drooped lower on her bosom. The door suddenly crashed shut, and she jumped in alarm and then sat down again. It must have been the wind, although the day had been very cold and still when she had entered the shed.

The pine smell brought faint memories of long-lost Christmases to mind, Christmases at the Squire's large cheerful house with the great yule log blazing and crackling on the hearth. Sometimes the chimney did not draw properly, and the east wind racing across the moors and down the old chimney would send puffs of pine smoke billowing into the room. She could almost smell it now.

She *could* smell it now!

Smoke!

As Annabelle stared at the piles of faggots on the other side of the shed, little snakes of smoke wound up from them and hung motionless in the cold air.

Poor Heckley, thought Annabelle. If I do not sound the alarm, all his work will be up in flames. She ran to the door—and found it securely locked and bolted from the outside.

With a feeling of panic she turned towards the smoke. Little tongues of flame were now crackling round the sticks of wood. She pulled them desperately aside in order to try to stamp the flames out, but her efforts only succeeded in making the blaze spread merrily. She began to scream and cry and batter at the door. The flames were between her and the only window.

How jolly a crackling fire sounds when a storm rages outside and the flames shoot merrily up the chimney. How terrifying, how nightmarish each crackle sounded now!

The heat was becoming intense. The smoke was suffocating. Annabelle felt herself falling, falling, and falling. Down and down and down into an endless pit of heat and smoke and flames.

ANNABELLE came back from a very long, long way away. "So you're here too—in hell, I mean," she murmured to Lady Jane whose face was staring down at her. Lady Jane let out an appropriately demonic shriek of laughter and Annabelle retreated into the pit.

When she regained consciousness again, she was lying in her own bed and a very concerned Lady Emmeline was perched on the edge of it.

"Now, be quiet, my dear," said Lady Emmeline. "The doctor will be here presently. You have had a very narrow escape. If Varleigh hadn't happened to be on the spot and rushed in and dragged you clear, you would have been roasted to a cinder. I must say I'm surprised at Varleigh. His coat was charred to bits and his hands all burned. I would have thought a man like him would have waited for one of the servants."

There was a soft footfall, and then Lord Varleigh's face was looking down at her. He took her hand in his own, and Annabelle noticed with surprise that her hands were bandaged as well as his. "How are you?" he said in a soft voice, smiling down at her in such a way that she felt she would faint again. "I think I am all right," she replied shyly. "I must thank you for saving my life."

"Oh, I always take care of my guests," he replied in a light mocking voice which belied the warmth of his eyes. For a long minute their eyes met and held as Lord Varleigh stared down at Annabelle in dawning surprise.

"I have something to do," he said abruptly. "I shall return presently to find out how you go on."

With that he marched to Lady Jane's room and gave her her marching orders in no uncertain terms, turning a deaf ear to every shriek and tear.

Lady Jane left.

Lord Varleigh kept wondering why he had not managed to be so firm with her before. It had all been so remarkably easy . . .

Chapter Ten

ANNABELLE WAS YOUNG and healthy and recovered quickly from her shock.

Lord Varleigh seemed more disposed to seek her company, but the Captain was constantly at her side. The fire in the pimping shed was decided to be an unfortunate accident and only Annabelle, with dark memories of Mad Meg's prophecy, was plagued with doubts.

Lord Varleigh's attentions to the three young ladies grew less as he joined more and more in the masculine pursuits of his gentlemen guests. Hopes began to wither and die in three feminine breasts, and their respective parents began peevishly to talk of going home.

In order to escape the increasingly unwelcome attentions of the Captain, Annabelle had taken to going for long walks. The Captain's heavy gallantry was laced with abject apologies for his behavior at Chiswick; he spoke so feverently of his love for Annabelle that she was half inclined to believe him and allowed him as much of her company as she felt she could bear.

Rising early from her bed one morning, Annabelle rose and stared out of the window across the great park. A light snow had fallen during the night and was now casting its blanket of stillness over the estates. Low leaden skies were swollen with the promise of more snow to come.

Lord Varleigh suddenly appeared just below her window. He had his gun on his shoulder and his dogs at his heels. He was alone.

Annabelle watched as he walked with easy athletic strides across the park in the direction of the woods. She had a sudden longing to join him, to have him to herself away from the jealous eyes and chatter of the other guests.

Without ringing for the maid, she dressed herself quickly in a new scarlet velvet walking dress and then pulled on a thick black pelisse lined with white ermine. Then she placed a poke bonnet on her head and tying the satin ribbons, surveyed herself with some pleasure in the glass. The exaggerated poke of the bonnet shaded her face in a most becoming way. She hoped Lord Varleigh would notice.

She ran downstairs and out into the park, her little half boots following the black imprint of Lord Varleigh's steps.

After about a mile of walking Annabelle began to feel ridiculous. Her outfit, which had seemed so becoming in the privacy of her bedroom, now appeared to her overdressed and fussy, more suitable for a walk down Bond Street than in these skeletal winter woods.

And after all, what would Lord Varleigh say if she did find him? She could not plead innocence—that she was simply wandering the woods at this unearthly hour in the morning at random. Her little footsteps followed Lord Varleigh's in a direct line. What if he should have that mocking look in his eye? What if he had gone to meet Lady Jane and Lady Jane's noisy dismissal from his home had all been playacting?

Doubts crowded one after the other into her mind till they seemed as gray and threatening as the lowering sky above. With a feeling of defeat, she began to retrace her steps and make the long journey back towards the great house.

Snow began to fall lightly over the deserted park which had a brooding, *waiting* feeling. I'm becoming as fanciful as old Meg, thought Annabelle with a shiver.

By the time she entered the great hall, she was feeling exhausted. Annabelle threw her hat and pelisse on a chair and went in search of Lady Emmeline. She had been avoiding her godmother of late as the old lady's eccentricity began to teeter on the edge of madness.

Lady Emmeline was kneeling at the prayer stool in the corner of her room. She was minus wig, and her bald pate gleamed in the livid light from the softly falling snow outside. She was wearing an old yellow nightgown with a brocade dressing gown lined with fur thrown over it. One of her frivolous high-heeled slippers had fallen off and lay on its side beside the prayer stool. Her eyes were shut and her lips were moving soundlessly.

Annabelle turned to leave.

"Don't go," said Lady Emmeline in a whisper. "Don't."

Annabelle paused, irresolute, in the doorway.

"You must join me," said Lady Emmeline, still in that eerie whisper. "We must prepare our souls for the afterlife."

"I shall leave you to the privacy of your devotions, Emmeline," said Annabelle, backing away and trying to make her own voice sound as normal as possible.

"I insist," said Lady Emmeline. "Come here, child."

So Annabelle wearily joined her. Lady Emmeline knelt at the prayer stool, and Annabelle knelt on the rug on the floor beside her. Lady Emmeline prayed for her immortal soul and poor Annabelle prayed for a normal life.

THE Honorable Caroline Dempsey looked down from her bedroom window and saw in the far distance Lord Varleigh emerging from the woods with his gun and his dogs. Caroline decided to wait for him in the hall and waylay him.

Despite her horsy appearance Caroline was more sensitive than her two rivals. She had been aware of a certain warmth of affection between Lord Varleigh and the pretty Annabelle and guessed that Annabelle was more of a force to be reckoned with than Lady Jane.

She paced up and down the hall, praying that her two rivals might not descend and steal a march on her with almost the same fervor that Lady Emmeline abovestairs was praying for her immortal soul. Caroline heard Mrs. O'Harold's laugh echoing along the corridor at the top of the stairs and the rapid sound of approaching footsteps. In the same moment she saw Annabelle's bonnet and pelisse lying over the chair. She quickly put them on and swung open the great door of the hall.

Powdery snow came swirling into the hall, but Caroline could still make out the figure of Lord Varleigh with his dogs at his side, still some distance away.

The approaching sound of Mrs. O'Harold's chattering voice spurred her to action.

Heedless of the damage to her thin silk slippers, Caroline plunged into the snow and ran towards Lord Varleigh.

There was a sudden report, awful to hear in all that white stillness.

The Honorable Caroline Dempsey stopped abruptly in her tracks and then dropped like a stone.

THE house party was at an end. Caroline's body had been removed for burial by her weeping parents, and searchers had combed the estate without success for signs of the marksman. It was at last decided by the local magistrate, who was tired of travelling in the wintry weather, that Caroline's death had been the unfortunate result of a stray bullet fired by a poacher. Only Annabelle wondered if the shot had been meant for herself.

She did not know who to confide in or who to trust. Perhaps Lord Varleigh's handsome face masked the brain of a madman. Perhaps one of her fellow guests was a murderer. The well-bred faces and high fluting voices began to seem sinister.

Two days after Caroline's funeral Annabelle was seated in the library, trying to read. Captain MacDonald came bustling in, suddenly seeming to Annabelle to appear comfortably normal with his fresh, handsome face and military side-whiskers.

"This place is giving me the Blues," he said robustly, placing one booted foot on the high fender and staring at Annabelle with a worried look on his face. "I don't like that 'accident.' I think there was something funny about it."

"I am feeling blue-devilled myself," said Annabelle. Her face was white, and she had large shadows under her eyes. She had a sudden longing to confide in somebody.

"Jimmy," she said. "Do sit down. I am in need of help."

The large Captain promptly sat down opposite her with his hands on his knees and stared at her with the affectionate expression of a large and devoted dog. "I'm the person to tell about it, Annabelle," he said.

Faltering at first and then with her voice growing stronger, she told the Captain of Mad Meg's warning, of her fears that the fire in the pimping shed had been deliberately set and that Caroline had been wearing her, Annabelle's, pelisse and bonnet when she had been shot.

"Odd," muttered the Captain, "Demned odd. Tell you what, Annabelle. I think it *might* just be coincidence, but why stay here, shaking in your shoes?"

"Emmeline is determined to stay," said Annabelle.

"Oh, no she won't. Not if I talk to her," said Captain MacDonald. "You go up to your rooms and tell your maid to pack your things, and I'll have us out of here in an hour. Get back to London, heh! Think of the theaters and the plays and you could come on some more drives with me if the weather ain't too bad. What a monster you must think me, Annabelle. After my terrible behavior at Chiswick. Don't really know why I did that. Must have been mad. Now come along . . . smile, that's a girl. Jimmy will look after you!"

Annabelle gave him a watery smile. She gratefully took his arm as he ushered her out into the hall.

"I say," said the Captain, "there ain't any hope of you and me tying the knot, is there? I mean to say," he added gruffly, shuffling his boots, "look after you, and all that. Very fond of you."

"I'm sorry. I just don't know," said Annabelle, looking searchingly up into his face. "I'm so frightened and everything seems so strange. Give me more time."

"All the time you want," said the Captain enthusiastically. "Be a good girl and give me a kiss and go off and see to your packing."

Annabelle shyly raised herself on tiptoe and kissed Captain Jimmy MacDonald on the cheek and scurried off upstairs.

Lord Varleigh slowly closed the study door on this

touching scene. He could not understand why he felt so unhappy.

EVERYONE seemed to revive in the sooty London air. Lady Emmeline seemed to have become her old self again, grotesquely dressed it is true, but no longer rambling and murmuring and praying for her soul. Annabelle flirted and danced with a great number of young men and felt that she was getting over that dangerous illness of being hopelessly in love with Lord Varleigh. If ever she found herself thinking about him, she resolutely concentrated on his inhuman "marriage mart" at Varleigh Court and the suspicious death of poor Caroline.

The Captain had not touched any liquor at all since his return, and his friends gloomily declared him to be a changed man and cast resentful glances at Annabelle.

As party and ridotto followed ball and breakfast, and the elegant figure of Lord Varleigh did not appear, Annabelle found the memory of him growing mercifully fainter. Her godmother had written to the rector praising the Captain in no uncertain terms, and the rector had written a pleading letter to Annabelle urging her not to throw over the love of a good man for some girlish romantic nonsense.

Annabelle became convinced that her own idea of love was wrong. Hurting and painful passion was no basis for a happy marriage, and what did one do when passion had fled? Mutual esteem and mutual interests were what mattered. And, indeed, the Captain did try. He even read books to please her and went so far as to remark that Miss Austen was a demned fine writer and Annabelle, who had caught him studying *Pride and Prejudice* forebore to point out that she had noticed the latest copy of the *Sporting Magazine* tucked between its gilt-edged pages.

One day Captain MacDonald turned up to take Annabelle out walking, wearing his full uniform. His fur cap was black with a red bag and a white bag over red plumes and gold cap lines ending in tassels and flounders. The jacket, dark blue with scarlet collar and cuffs, had silver cords on the front. The pelisse, dark blue like the jacket, was laced with silver in the same way with a black fur edging. White breeches and black Hessian boots edged with silver braid with silver tassels in front; a sword belt made of crimson leather and ornamented with silver embroidery completed the ensemble. Annabelle thought he looked magnificent and told him so, and the large Captain smiled at her almost shyly and twiddled his side-whiskers with one large hand.

As they walked along Piccadilly, Annabelle was pleasurably aware of the admiring glances cast in their direction, but she had almost bumped full into Lady Jane Cherle before she noticed her.

Lady Jane was all that was gracious. She greeted Annabelle like an old friend. Lady Jane explained she was sending out cards for a dinner party and Annabelle *must* come. Annabelle was about to give a polite refusal when, to her dismay, she heard the Captain accepting the invitation for both of them.

"How *could* you, Jimmy?" demanded Annabelle when Lady Jane had left them. "Lady Jane is a *cat*."

"Oh, she's all right," said the Captain amiably. "Bit *fast* I admit, but quite the thing for all that."

For the umpteenth time Annabelle pondered over the vagaries of society. If she, Annabelle, had behaved even a tiny little bit as scandalously as Lady Jane, then all the doors of the top houses would be slammed in her face. But for some reason Lady Jane was accepted everywhere. "Almost as if society felt in need of a resident whore," thought Annabelle and then blushed painfully as she realised she had voiced her thought aloud.

"Here! I say!" said the Captain in alarm. "Shouldn't talk like that, you know. Not the thing!"

Annabelle fell silent. She could only hope Lady Emmeline would forbid her to go.

But her godmother was depressingly enthusiastic. "If you were strictly a debutante, I wouldn't let you," explained the old lady. "But you're going with Jimmy, and Jane's careful of her reputation at her dinners. You'll meet only the top people there."

It certainly seemed a sedate enough gathering. Admittedly the Captain's admirers were present in the shape of Major Timothy Wilks and George Louch, but apart from teasing the Captain over his sobriety, which was the talk of London, they seemed more subdued than usual.

Lady Jane's house in Manchester Square was in the first style of elegance with Egyptian rooms and Etruscan rooms and powdered, liveried footmen.

Her fortune had been gathered from two late husbands who had had the good taste to die shortly after their marriages. It was rumored that although Lady Jane had more than enough money of her own, she greedily collected what she could from her current lovers. Society had watched with bated breath for the replacement to Lord Varleigh, but so far it seemed as if Lady Jane intended to remain heart free.

Annabelle was reluctantly forced to admit that Lady Jane was a good hostess. Her chef was excellent and her vintages of the best. She said she had heard Captain Jimmy was as sober as a judge these days and instructed a footman to serve him with lemonade.

Annabelle eyed the handsome Captain approvingly.

He had certainly been a model escort of late. He was a . . . well, a *comfortable* kind of man. He seemed to be relishing his lemonade as if it were the best vintage Burgundy.

"By Jove, this is good," he said. "You chaps ought to try it. Not in the common way, you know. Faint taste of liquorice or something. Gives it a fresh taste."

And Lady Jane, who had spiked the Captain's lemonade with arrack, gave him her beautiful smile and relaxed in her high carved chair at the end of the table while she waited for the inevitable results.

Mr. Louch began to describe the expertise of a juggler he had seen at Vauxhall Gardens the previous summer. "Didn't throw balls or clubs or anything like that in the air," he said. "But everything else. Champagne bottles, knives, forks. He kept them all up in the air at the same time. The man's a wizard! I thought you were good at that regimental dinner, Jimmy, but you ain't a patch on this fellow."

"Bet you I am," said the Captain wrathfully, taking a long pull at his lemonade goblet. "Bet you anything you like!"

"Bet you a monkey," tittered Mr. Louch.

"Done!" cried the Captain, shaking off Annabelle's little hand from his sleeve.

"Can't you *do* something," cried Annabelle to her hostess as the Captain began to gather an assortment of objects in front of him.

Lady Jane said nothing, but she lay back in her chair and smiled like a cat.

Annabelle turned back wildly to the Captain. "Please, Jimmy," she begged. "Don't make a fool of yourself."

"Leave me alone," said Captain MacDonald huffily. "We ain't married yet."

Annabelle flushed crimson with mortification as he got to his feet. In his large hands he held a champagne bottle, a knife, a silver salt cellar, and a wine glass.

He began to throw them up in the air, deftly catching them and recirculating them as the guests cheered and laughed.

"Here, *catch*!" called Lady Jane—and threw an orange down the table in the direction of the Captain.

He saw it coming and took his eyes off the juggling objects for a split second in order to try and catch it. The champagne bottle crashed onto the silver epergne in the middle of the table and was followed by the wine glass. Both splintered into fragments. The silver salt cellar hurtled into the plate of syllabub in front of Annabelle and splashed the contents of the dessert over her dress, and the knife fell down and gashed the Captain on the cheek.

"That wasn't playing fair," howled the enraged Captain. "Bet's off!"

Annabelle reached forward and slowly picked up the Captain's lemonade glass.

She took a sip of its contents and put it down. She rose to her feet.

She turned and faced Lady Jane who sat laughing at the end of the table.

"You have put arrack in the Captain's lemonade, Lady Jane."

In a louder voice Annabelle repeated, "You put arrack in Captain MacDonald's lemonade. A *shabby* trick."

A silence fell on the rest of the guests and only the drunken Captain who was trying to balance a knife on his nose seemed unconcerned.

Now Lady Jane could flaunt her amours over half of London and still be good *ton*. But to spike a man's drink was like cheating at cards.

"Don't all look at me like that," shrilled Lady Jane. "'Twas a joke, no more."

Annabelle rose from the table and left without a backward glance. She was shortly followed by most of the guests. The Captain remained at his place with a silly smile on his face. "'Strordinarily good champagne, Lady Jane," he said dreamily.

"Go to hell," said Lady Jane, throwing a glass at him which missed and struck the opposite wall.

"Very well, ma'am," said the Captain with awful dignity.

He tottered out into the hall and called for his carriage. He was politely informed that he had arrived with Miss Quennell in Lady Emmeline's carriage and that Miss Quennell had already departed in it.

His good temper rapidly evaporating, the Captain hailed a hack and directed it to Berkeley Square. He was already seething in its evil-smelling interior by the time he arrived at Lady Emmeline's house. He had every intention of giving Miss Annabelle Quennell a piece of his mind. She would have to learn to take a joke or he would take his riding crop to her—after they were married of course.

He strode heavily into the hall to see Annabelle mounting the stairs. He unceremoniously dragged her down again and gave her a shake.

"It's time you learned what's what, my girl," he grated. "Do you think it fair to me that you prim up like a Methodist any time I'm having fun. Be demned to you, miss." With that he dragged her into his arms and ruthlessly kissed her. He smelled overpoweringly of arrack and cigars and his lips were hot and wet.

Annabelle pushed him away. She was trembling with rage. "You make me sick," she said in a shaking voice, and turning on her heel, she mounted the steps, again trying not to run.

"I do, do I?" yelled the Captain. "Well, you'll be sorry you said that, Miss Annabelle Quennell. You'll be sorry. . . ."

Chapter Eleven

ANNABELLE QUENNELL WAS going home—just as soon as spring came and the roads were fit for travel.

Lady Emmeline had ranted and raved, but for once Annabelle remained unmoved. Annabelle felt she had disgraced herself completely. Lady Emmeline had accused her of "leading Jimmy on," and Annabelle with her cheeks aflame had had to admit the truth of the accusation.

The Captain himself had heaped coals of fire on her head by calling the next morning to apologise most humbly for his behavior and to accept her final and most definite rejection of his suit with forgiving good humor.

Despite all Annabelle's hopes for a speedy departure, winter kept its grip on England, and by the beginning of March London was experiencing the coldest and hardest frosts in living memory. The great families were slowly returning to Town to start elaborate preparations for yet another Season, and once again, the flambeaux blazed outside the Mayfair mansions and carriages jammed the Ring in Hyde Park on a Sunday afternoon.

Only the bravest dared to venture out in the new Spring muslins, and one young hopeful contracted rheumatic fever by damping her skirts when the temperatures were below zero.

Annabelle attended a few routs and parties in the

company of Lady Emmeline. The Captain was often present and often unsnubbable. Annabelle no longer felt at ease in his company after his onslaught in the hall. Lady Emmeline could pooh-pooh for all she was worth and call Annabelle missish, but as far as Miss Annabelle Quennell was concerned, she would now rather die a spinster than be wed to the Captain.

He had an endearing boyish charm when he was sober, but Annabelle noticed that since Lady Jane's party, he only managed to stay sober during the day. Lady Emmeline might point out acidly that in this year of 1815, that in itself was a great achievement. But the other bucks and bloods held their wine better—in the company of ladies at least—and did not seem disposed to dance on the ledge of their box at the opera or to juggle with the silverware at dinner.

But Annabelle had found a new interest which effectively took her mind off the Captain's erratic behavior.

Skating was the rage this winter, and everyone who was anyone was giving a skating party. Annabelle loved them. They were gay and exciting and much more exhilarating than parties held in overcrowded and overheated rooms.

One day, when Annabelle was upstairs in her rooms adding the finishing touches to a dashing skating costume to be worn at the Egremonts' party that evening, the Captain called on Lady Emmeline and demanded a few words with her in private.

More grotesquely painted and gowned than ever, Lady Emmeline received him in the drawing room.

The Captain went straight to the point. "It's about Annabelle," he said, pacing up and down. "One minute it's on and the next it's off. What's happening?"

"It looks as if she's made up her mind to go home," said Lady Emmeline sadly. "I'll miss her."

The Captain looked at her with some impatience. "Well, I'm glad you got something out of it. After all, she's cost you a pretty penny as it is."

"She has amused me and kept me young and furthermore she's saved my life," said Lady Emmeline with quaint dignity.

"Quite," said the Captain, fingering his side-whiskers. "But I mean to say, since she won't have me, it's not as if she'll get your money."

"Don't be vulgar," snapped the Dowager Marchioness.

"Oh, for heaven's sake . . . I mean, you've known me from the cradle," said Captain MacDonald. "You ain't going to go cutting me out of your will."

"You're in my will . . . somewhere," said Lady Emmeline drily, "and for your further information, I have no intention of dying for a great many years."

"Of course, of course," said the Captain hurriedly, and with that he had to be content.

DARKNESS fell on the old buildings of Lincoln's Inn. Lawyers, solicitors, and clerks had at last gone home. With the agility of a cat a dark figure slid up the old brick wall to the windows of Messrs. Crindle and Bridge. There was a sharp cracking noise, and the figure flattened itself against the wall.

There was silence except for the faint cry of the watch. Another crack and the window opened, and the dark figure slid over the sill like a shadow.

As he held the stump of a candle over the piles of papers and boxes, the flame wavered backwards and forwards, the light eventually coming to rest on a long black box with the name Eversley stamped on the front.

A silver-barrelled pistol appeared in strong hands lit by the candlelight. With a sharp crack the butt was brought down on the hasp of the box.

"Now," whispered a voice in the darkness. "Now, dear Emmeline, Dowager Marchioness of Eversley, we shall see what we shall see . . ."

"WE can't wait around for Jimmy any more," snapped Lady Emmeline. "We may as well get started. Horley, bring our skates."

It was a fine clear moonlit night. The Egremonts' skating party was to be held at the side of a small lake on the Chiswick road. A bleak winter sun had thawed the sooty snow on the roofs earlier in the day, and now long, wicked-looking icicles hung over the streets.

At times like this, reflected Annabelle, she was almost sorry to be going home. There would be no more parties or balls once she was safely back in the rectory, suffering the lash of her mother's sharp tongue. Bit by bit Annabelle was remembering her home life more clearly instead of the unreal dream picture of warmth and safety she had conjured up in her mind.

But go she must. She had encouraged the Captain. Looking back on her year in London, she found it all had an air of unreality. She had tried to do her duty as far as her mother and Lady Emmeline were concerned, and look where it had led! For the first time in her young life Annabelle realised she had a duty to herself. Let her mother rant and rave and say she had ruined her chances and the chances of her sisters. Her duty did not lie in making a distasteful marriage.

The little lake was lit with brightly colored lanterns strung through the trees. The lake itself gleamed like beaten silver, vanishing off into a long silver alley which was the small frozen stream which fed it. Tables had been set up beside the lake, the powdered and liveried footmen stamping their feet and blowing on their white-gloved hands to keep warm.

The chatter was all about the weather. They knew it couldn't possibly last, but while it did, everyone was determined to enjoy the latest skating rage. A German band played cheerful waltzes, and the exotic smells of food from the buffet tables set up beside the ice mingled with the perfumes of the ladies.

Annabelle had made her curtsy to Lord and Lady Egremont and had allowed Horley to help her on with her skates. She was standing on the edge of the ice wondering whether to launch off herself or wait for a partner when she suddenly saw Sylvester Varleigh.

He was skating rapidly towards her and as he came nearer, Annabelle saw he was regarding her with a strange tenderness and warmth which altered the habitually austere lines of his face.

She half turned—unbelieving—expecting to see Lady Jane or some other dasher standing behind her. But, no. Lord Varleigh's warmth was all for her alone.

He silently took her gloved hands in his and led her onto the ice.

"I've missed you, Miss Quennell," he said quietly, and Annabelle's heart gave a dizzy lurch. All the barriers she had set up against him melted away before that single sentence.

The reflection of the lights bobbed and danced dizzily on the ice under feet. Far above the stars wheeled drunkenly in their courses as Annabelle hung onto Lord Varleigh's hands and wished never to let go.

Skating faster and faster, he swept her far away to the other side of the lake which was empty and deserted. Still holding her hands, he drew her down onto a fallen log at the edge of the lake. There seemed to be so much they had to say—there suddenly seemed to be so little they had to say.

His eyes glinted strangely in the moonlight as he bent his head towards hers.

Annabelle closed her eyes as his lips came down on hers, pressing deeper and deeper, becoming more and more exploring until the pleasure and passion became almost a pain, and she clung to him, drunkenly and dizzily, freeing her hands only to clasp them behind his neck and draw him closer.

His long white fingers slid under the fur of her mantle and began to caress her breast, and Annabelle stiffened in fright and trembled and then with a little sigh turned her face up to him again.

"Annabelle! *Annabelle*!" Lady Emmeline's voice echoed across the ice, and Lord Varleigh gently released Annabelle. Smiling gently into her eyes, he straightened her bonnet. "Run along," he said softly, "and see what it is she wants. And then come back to me. Or I shall come looking for you."

With her face glowing and her eyes like the stars above, Annabelle flew across the long expanse of ice to where Lady Emmeline was teetering inexpertly on her skates.

"Annabelle!" she cried. "We have been looking everywhere for you."

The "we," Annabelle noticed with a sinking heart, was Lady Emmeline and Captain Jimmy MacDonald.

"I'll leave you two young things together," said Lady Emmeline with her usual irritating giggle, and she waddled off rapidly on her skates towards the buffet, leaving them standing together.

"I c-can't speak to you just now, Jimmy," faltered Annabelle, straining her eyes to the far side of the lake where Lord Varleigh was waiting for her.

"I'm *surprised* at you, Annabelle," said the Captain reprovingly. "Allowing a fellow like Varleigh to kiss you like that! He's always sitting around kissing girls at parties, but it's usually women like Lady Jane, not respectable debutantes. He must think you are *fast*."

"He d-doesn't . . . I d-didn't . . . ," stammered Annabelle, while all the time her mind raced and raced. Lord Varleigh had not said he loved her or wished to marry her. The fact that he had said he missed her did not add up to a proposal of marriage. She felt cold and betrayed and miserable. What did she know of this social world anyway? A world where lip service only was paid to the moral code and the only crime was to be found out.

She dismally became aware that the Captain was skating her off towards where the river wound away through the trees and that her skates were following him with all the mindless action of a clockwork toy.

She was too confused and upset and miserable to notice that he was leading her very far away from the party indeed.

The flat frozen river grew narrower and narrower and darker and darker as the trees almost met overhead, the moonlight sending their skeletal shadows crisscrossing across the ice.

Annabelle tugged at Jimmy's large hands in a sudden attempt to free herself. He seemed like a large stranger, and she began to wonder whether she knew him at all. He finally stopped and spun her round to face him. She could not make out his expression as his face was in the shadows of the overhanging trees.

"I'm sorry about this," he said in a serious voice. "Emmeline left you all her money, you see. She won't live long. I decided I was wasting my time trying to kill her. Now, if you had married me, as your husband I would have had control of your fortune. But you wouldn't. Not you. But you had the luck of the devil.

First Varleigh drags you from that shed and then that poor bitch Caroline took the bullet that was meant for you."

Annabelle wrestled desperately and futilely in his arms. "Th-this is one o-of y-your mad jokes," she stammered wildly.

"Joke!" he laughed, giving her an almost absentminded little shake. "That's a good one. I've never been more serious in my life."

"You killed Caroline," whispered Annabelle, ceasing her struggles as the full enormity of what he was saying penetrated her frightened brain.

"Quiet, while I tell you. I must tell you," he went on in that calm, serious voice. "I watched you very carefully. Thought we were going to tie the knot after all. Then you said I made you sick. Now you shouldn't have done that, Annabelle. That was naughty, especially when a man has every dun in London banging on his knocker.

"So I broke into Emmeline's lawyers' office and read the will. If you die, I'm next in line to inherit. And why? What a joke! The irony of it! You were to get the money for saving the old girl's life when I was trying to kill her. Rich, isn't it? But for that, you wouldn't have seen a penny of it once you had turned me down.

"So now you've got to die. I hope you understand, Annabelle," he went on in an earnest, almost boyish voice. "I've got my reputation as an officer and a gentleman to consider."

"What are you going to do to me?" whispered Annabelle.

"This," he said.

He gave her a sharp push. She catapulted backwards across the ice and tumbled headlong into a jagged hole of black water.

"Nicely done. Very nicely done," said the Captain

appreciatively as Annabelle's bonnet disappeared beneath the water. "I thought I'd never be able to hack through that ice in time."

He moved slowly forward on his skates. Annabelle's pathetic little hand emerged and scrabbled at the jagged edge of the ice. Almost lazily he pried it loose with the toe of his skate.

"I hope she's not going to take too long," he muttered to himself. "It's demned cold."

Once again Annabelle surfaced and let out a watery scream, and the Captain sighed with impatience. Then he swung round with an oath as he heard an answering cry and heard the hiss of skates racing towards him across the ice.

Lord Varleigh came speeding towards him with all the velocity of the bullet that had killed Caroline Dempsey. The Captain put up his fist, but Lord Varleigh had gained double his strength through fear and rage. He dodged under the Captain's guard and planted the best flush hit of his life right on the point of the Captain's chin.

Captain Jimmy MacDonald hit the ice with an almighty crash and lay still.

Lord Varleigh seized a dead branch from the bank and, lying flat on his stomach, muttering prayers and curses, he edged towards the hole. Annabelle, making a last desperate effort, felt the branch somehow with her numbed fingers and held on. Sliding right up to the edge of the hole and praying that the ice would hold, Lord Varleigh slid his arms into the water and under her armpits and then held on like grim death while he hallooed and shouted for help. His arms were rapidly turning numb with the cold and Annabelle had fallen unconscious—he hoped—and was swaying limply in them, her head just above the icy water, looking as white and as pale as the indifferent moon above.

Just when he felt he could stand the strain no longer, he heard the blessed sounds of answering shouts. Soon he was surrounded by a crowd of guests and footmen. Willing hands helped him to support Annabelle, ropes were brought to tie up the Captain, and ladders were brought to place across the hole. All the while Lady Emmeline teetered and squawked, "It can't be true. Not Jimmy. It can't be true."

Annabelle was wrapped in blankets, hot fiery drinks were poured down her throat, and slowly her large eyes fluttered open.

The watching members of the *ton* gave a great sigh. Was it relief? Or was it disappointment?

After all, it would have made a far better piece of gossip had she died.

Chapter Twelve

ON THE SAME evening a more international drama was taking place.

At the Congress of Vienna the tinkling sleigh parties drove nightly home from the Wienerwald, and the music of a succession of balls, concerts, tableaux vivants and masques kept the reelected statesmen in their powdered wigs and silk-covered calves too busy to pay any attention to the threatening rumors from France.

On March 7 while Vienna prepared for another great ball and the Czar of All the Russias spent a pleasant afternoon judging which of two ladies could dress the quickest—one managing the process in a minute and a quarter and the other in a minute and fifty seconds—a courier arrived at Metternich's house with dispatches from Genoa. The Chancellor was too tired from the exhausting combination of business and revelry to open them directly.

After resting for a while on his couch, he felt once again strong enough to deal with affairs of state. And he opened the dispatch.

Napoleon had escaped from Elba. The Sovereigns of Europe, assembled in Vienna, had been too busy to pay attention to that one ever-present threat. And they had let the Corsican ogre escape from his cage.

IN Berkeley Square, while Annabelle Quennell tossed and turned in a feverish sleep upstairs, Lord Varleigh paced Lady Emmeline's drawing room and dealt with a diplomatic problem of his own.

Lady Emmeline had hysterically protested that Annabelle's near drowning had been an accident. Lord Varleigh's servants had placed the bound Captain in Lady Emmeline's cellars while their master tried to make the Dowager Marchioness see sense. Lord Varleigh did not know of the Captain's other attempts at murder or that he had been responsible for Caroline Dempsey's death. He only knew that Captain Jimmy MacDonald, for some inexplicable reason, had tried to stop him from rescuing Annabelle. In his opinion the Captain should stand trial for attempted murder.

Lady Emmeline wept and pleaded. She had no son of her own, she said. Jimmy was like a son to her. She would die if anything happened to him.

In despair Lord Varleigh sent a footman to rout out the Captain's Colonel.

Colonel James Ward-Price was a clever man on the field of battle and incredibly stupid in peacetime. He loved and admired Captain Jimmy MacDonald as standing for everything the perfect soldier should be. Lord Varleigh could not have sent for a worse judge.

The Colonel insisted on hearing Captain Jimmy MacDonald's version of the story.

The Captain was led into the room with his hands behind his back. He looked as if he were about to face a firing squad and he indeed thought the game was up.

The first glimmer of hope he had was when Lady Emmeline rushed to him and threw her pudgy arms round his great body and smeared rouge and gray powder on his chest. She was weeping and exclaiming over his bound hands and blaming Lord Varleigh for his "inhuman treatment."

Then his Colonel ordered the footmen to unbind him and told him in a kindly gruff voice to sit down and tell them what it was all about because Miss Quennell was in a heavily sedated and feverish sleep.

That sulky, brooding, almost childish look that Lord Varleigh remembered came over the Captain's face and he leaned forward in the chair provided for him, his hands on his knees and began to talk earnestly.

"Look, it's like this. There's no use me trying to say I haven't behaved badly because I have. Annabelle had just told me finally that she was going home and didn't want to have anything to do with me. I had seen her earlier kissing Varleigh and taxed her with it. She laughed in my face and said Varleigh was another rake and she had been leading him on just in order to tease him but that it didn't matter anyway because she was quitting London and she would never see him again either. Seems she's got a tendre for some chap in Yorkshire and she prefers him to all of us."

"Go on," said Lord Varleigh. His face was very white.

"Well . . . she fell backwards into this hole in the ice. I was as mad as fire with her, and I thought I would let her have a dunking to teach her a lesson. Then right at that moment, you arrived on the scene, Varleigh, and I was jealous of you. I could still see you and Annabelle kissing and caressing in my mind's eye. Oh, God!" The Captain groaned and buried his head in his hands. There was a shocked silence.

Both Lady Emmeline and Colonel Ward-Price were convinced that he was telling the truth. Lord Varleigh thought that if he weren't, then it was a consummate piece of acting.

But Captain Jimmy MacDonald had just remembered

that the broken window and deed box would be discovered in the morning when Lady Emmeline's lawyers returned to work—hence the realistic groan.

The Colonel cleared his throat. "Don't take on so, my boy," he said, placing his hand awkwardly on the Captain's shoulder. "You behaved disgracefully, of course, and apologies are certainly the order of the day. But I don't think any of us in this room could find it in his or her heart to prosecute. I . . . what is it, man?"

An officer had bustled unceremoniously into the room and handed him a sealed letter. The Colonel broke it open and gave an exclamation.

"Napoleon has escaped!" he said. "He is even now believed to be in France marshalling his troops.

"Come, my boy," he said, helping the Captain to his feet. "Your duty is clear. You will fight for your country once more. I am sure, my lord, you would not wish to see one of England's finest soldiers in chains at a moment like this. Come, my lord, you have served with distinction yourself!"

Lord Varleigh looked thoughtfully at the Captain. After all, all the criminal riffraff of the taverns and gutters would once more be marching to war as well. Most of them were better employed on the field of battle.

"Very well," he said.

"I say . . . thanks awfully, old man," said the Captain boyishly. "I can't . . ."

"You must not see Miss Quennell again," said Lord Varleigh, "or communicate with her in any way."

"Of course. *Of course*!" cried Captain MacDonald, jumping up and wringing Lord Varleigh's hand enthusiastically.

"Come, my boy," said the Colonel. "We have work to do!"

Lady Emmeline clung to the Captain, crying and sobbing and had to be pried loose.

For the hundredth time the old lady wondered if Annabelle realised the prize she had let slip through her hands.

What a man!

Chapter Thirteen

THE BRAVE SOLDIERS marched to war, and one of them at least went away with a light heart.

Captain Jimmy MacDonald could not believe his luck. The lawyers had obviously not reported the break-in to Lady Emmeline. Now the prospect of a glorious battle and possible promotion lay in front of him. And when it was all over, there would be plenty of time to seek out Miss Quennell and put a period to her irritating existence.

Lord Varleigh sat in his town house and listened to the fifes and drums and trumpets of the soldiers. He himself had seen enough of the horrors of war and had fought bravely in the Peninsular Campaign. But it was not the sound of the marching armies which depressed him so. It was MacDonald's remarks to the effect that Annabelle had only been teasing when she had let him kiss her so warmly.

Women were the devil! Heartless, fickle, and avaricious. At least Lady Jane had only wanted his money to play with. Annabelle Quennell had wanted his heart, and she had very nearly managed to secure it. Damn her! He would never see her again.

And, Annabelle, weak and listless after her fever, tossed and turned on her bed and wondered why Lord Varleigh had not called or even left a message.

For the first time Lady Emmeline was beginning to find Annabelle a bore. With her splendid looks faded with her illness and her listless air, Annabelle no longer fed Lady Emmeline's aging spirits with her air of ebullient youth. Lady Emmeline dreamed frequently of the handsome Captain and sighed pleasurably over his outrageous behavior. If *she* had been the one who had been kidnapped and taken to Chiswick . . . ah, then, what a different story! As Lady Emmeline entered into another bout of prolonged eccentricity, she once again dressed herself in debutante clothes and greedily studied all the cases she could where an older woman had married a younger man.

By the time Annabelle was well enough to venture downstairs, she was met with a chilly reception. In Lady Emmeline's mad mind Annabelle was now a rival for the Captain's affections.

That's why I wasted all this time and money on the chit! thought Lady Emmeline with a rare burst of sane honesty. I'm in love with Jimmy myself!

Annabelle's quiet request that she should be allowed to go home was met with enthusiasm by her hostess. Arrangements were made for Annabelle to use Lady Emmeline's travelling chariot but no mention was made of any money to be given to her for her journey. Annabelle could only be glad that she had had the foresight to furnish Madame Croke with a whole folio of spring designs.

Annabelle quickly recovered her glowing looks and good health but that only sufficed to add fuel to Lady Emmeline's growing dislike and jealousy.

One day shortly before Annabelle was due to journey North, Lady Emmeline had abruptly ordered her to go to Bond Street and had furnished her with a shopping list and the reluctant Horley as escort.

Lady Emmeline watched until Annabelle's sickeningly jaunty bonnet had turned the corner of Berkeley Square and then ordered her town carriage to be brought round. The Dowager Marchioness was going to pay a visit to her solicitors, Messrs. Crindle and Bridge. Annabelle Quennell with her missish airs should not have her money. It should go to Captain Jimmy one way or the other. If the Captain married her—oh, blissful thought!—then he would have her money anyway. And if she died . . . Lady Emmeline looked round the sunny streets from the darkness of her carriage and shuddered. Impossible thought! She felt as if she would live forever.

Mr. Robert Crindle, the senior partner, did not look as honored and delighted to see the Dowager Marchioness as he usually did. In fact, thought Lady Emmeline in surprise, he looked furtive and guilty.

No matter. "I want to see my will," said Lady Emmeline.

Mr. Crindle put his chalky nails together and sighed. "Then you have heard," he said. "A most regrettable incident. I did not report it because I thought it was some felon searching for jewels. Some of these uneducated criminals seem to think we keep our clients' jewels in our deed boxes."

"What on earth are you drivelling on about?" snapped Lady Emmeline.

Mr. Crindle gave an even deeper sigh. "So you did not know after all. But I had better tell you just the same. Someone broke into this office on Wednesday night and cracked open the box containing your documents. Whoever it was left the copies of your ladyship's will lying crumpled on the floor, but mark my words, the fellow was looking for jewels. Of course I reported the

147

matter to the Runners and I . . ."

His voice faded in Lady Emmeline's ears as her old mind worked furiously. One thought piled on top of the other. Annabelle's insistence that Jimmy had been trying to kill her so he could inherit. Annabelle's fevered babblings about the death of Caroline Dempsey. Annabelle's horror of learning that the Captain had been forgiven. Annabelle's scream that they had all gone mad. All put down to the feverish ramblings of a sick girl. And now this! That Wednesday had been the night of the skating party. What she was thinking was dreadful. It could not be true!

". . . left no clues," went on Mr. Crindle's voice, suddenly breaking into Lady Emmeline's tortured thoughts, "except this. It shows the felon must have been robbing other places earlier in the evening."

He held out something which winked and glittered in the dim light of the musty office. Lady Emmeline stared at it and bit back an exclamation.

It was the diamond stickpin she had given Jimmy as an engagement present.

"Enough of this matter," Mr. Crindle was saying. "Did you wish to alter your will, my lady?"

"Yes," said Lady Emmeline hoarsely, getting unsteadily to her feet. "Leave the lot to m'parrot. See you about it another time. Not well. Not well at all."

Lady Emmeline sat helplessly in her carriage, bitter tears cutting through the paint and powder on her cheeks. If only she were a man! She wanted revenge. She thought of the way the Captain had led her along and fooled her and groaned aloud. She prayed for a quick and merciful death for herself and a long and painful one for the Captain.

Varleigh! That was it. He should revenge her. He would see justice done. Lady Emmeline directed her carriage to Lord Varleigh's town house and then leaned her head back against the squabs, feeling as if she would die from humiliation.

She was to receive another blow. Lord Varleigh had left for Varleigh Court only that morning. She gave a groan and the footman looked at her anxiously and asked her if she would care to leave a message.

"Message, that's it," said Lady Emmeline faintly. "Show me to a room; bring me brandy and writing materials—in that order."

The footman went off to fetch them, shaking his powdered head. He was new to service which was why he had been left in London with a skeleton staff while his more important colleagues journeyed to Varleigh Court. His name was John Ferguson, a Scot of almost ridiculously handsome looks. He returned with the brandy decanter and paper and ink to find Lady Emmeline standing over at the fireplace of Lord Varleigh's study, looking at herself in the looking glass and scrubbing the paint from her withered features with a dirty pocket handkerchief.

"I look an old fright," sobbed Lady Emmeline.

John Ferguson stood on one foot and then the other. He did not know what to say.

He had already been warned several times about his free and easy speech. But the old girl seemed to be in such distress that she looked ill. Also she looked more approachable with the muck off her face. But he stood silent, waiting for his orders.

Lady Emmeline sat down at a desk and began to write. "I want you to see that this is sent express to Lord Varleigh," she said over her shoulder.

"Yes, my lady," said John Ferguson dutifully.

Lady Emmeline finished at last and sanded the parchment and sealed it. She turned to hand it to the footman and once again the tears poured from her eyes.

John looked at her helplessly. "Oh, don't take on so,"

he said at last. "A charming and elegant lady like yourself should not cry."

Lady Emmeline blinked and brought him into focus for the first time. Brilliant blue eyes fringed with thick, almost feminine black lashes looked down into her own. "Thank you," she said faintly. "May I have some of that brandy? I have had the most terrible shock."

She admired the footman's tall figure as he deftly poured the spirits into a goblet. Lady Emmeline drained it at one gulp. "A terrible shock," she repeated, looking at him more hopefully this time.

John carefully took his cue. "It is not my place to question my betters, my lady," he said cautiously. "But sometimes it makes the heart easier if you talk about it—even if the listener is only a servant like myself."

Lady Emmeline needed no further encouragement. She burst out into a long garbled tale of the Captain's iniquities while the footman tut-tutted and refilled her glass in a most reassuring manner.

She finally paused and looked coyly up at the footman from under the meager spikes of her wet eyelashes. "You must think me an incredible old fool," she said.

It was then that John Ferguson, with one bold stroke of Gaelic genius, secured his own future.

"It seems to me," he said, "as if Captain MacDonald was secretly in love with you himself, my lady, and your trying to marry him off to someone else fair turned his mind."

What an intelligent young man! How acute—how *sharp* of him to have hit upon the truth.

An hour of delicious conversation later and John Ferguson had agreed to move to Lady Emmeline's employ. Lady Emmeline gave a fleeting thought to her parrot, but what could a bird do with money anyway. Of Annabelle Quennell she thought not at all.

* * *

ANNABELLE was promenading her grieving heart past the elegant shop windows of Bond Street. Her life had taken on the unreal quality of a nightmare. It slowly dawned on her that Lord Varleigh was not going to call and that he had actually *forgiven* Captain Jimmy MacDonald for outright murder. Perhaps he hadn't understood. Did he not realise that Jimmy would try again? Annabelle remembered what the Captain had said about Lady Emmeline's will. She would have a quiet talk with her godmother when she returned and *beg* the old lady to cut her out of her will or she, Annabelle, would never know a day's rest again. Annabelle shuddered despite the warmth of the spring day as she recalled several on-dits of the previous Season. Lord Jarston's wife had been unfaithful to him, and he had taken her off to his country estate where she had mysteriously died. The pretty heiress, Belinda Thompson, who had appeared to have a tremendous love of life, had inexplicably thrown herself to her death from her bedroom window leaving an impoverished distant cousin of questionable morals to inherit her wealth. Of course society said and believed the worst, but nothing was ever done about it. Every time Annabelle saw a figure in uniform, she shied nervously.

She bought presents for her family, silks and ribbons for the girls, a jar of fine snuff for her father, and a silver vinaigrette and a box of Indian muslin handkerchiefs for her mother.

Then she walked slowly back to Berkeley Square, bracing herself for the interview with her godmother.

But Lady Emmeline had dismissed Captain Jimmy MacDonald entirely from her mind. The old lady felt she had been fooled and that had hurt more than the Captain's criminal behavior. She remarked rather testily that she had no longer any intention of leaving Annabelle any money since the girl had shown herself unwilling to be wed and added blithely that she hoped Annabelle would have a safe and speedy journey North.

Her indifference and uncaring cruelty hurt the gentle and sensitive Annabelle who had begun to grow fond of the old lady.

With the fine spring weather it was now safe to travel. There was nothing left for Annabelle to do but to start on her long journey home. She would never wed. She would remain a spinster until the end of her days, mourning over her foolish misplaced sense of duty which had made her tolerate the Captain's attentions and her inexperience which had made her encourage the amorous uncaring advances of a heartless rake.

Chapter Fourteen

SPRING CAME LATE to the Yorkshire moors. April had been a cold and stormy month with great gray clouds trailing across the hills and icy winds blasting through every crack and cranny of the rectory.

Once Annabelle's welcome home—if it could be called a welcome—had passed, life had almost gone back to its old familiar pattern of housework and calls on her father's parishoners.

Annabelle's tale of the iniquities of Captain Mac-Donald and the eccentricity of Lady Emmeline had been met by sullen jealous silence on the part of her sisters who felt sure *they* would not have made a mess of such opportunities and by unconcealed impatience on the part of Mrs. Quennell who felt that Annabelle had imagined the whole thing and said so in no uncertain terms. Only her gentle father had been horrified in the extreme, and despite his wife's acid tongue, he had written a very severe letter to Lady Emmeline.

Annabelle's fine new wardrobe had been turned over to her sisters. Mary and Susan would soon be making their come-out at the Harrogate assemblies and such finery was wasted on Annabelle who had proved to be such a disappointment.

*　　*　　*

ONE day when the scrubby grass of the meadows round the rectory was blooming with purple clover and the wild garlic was just beginning to break through its green sheaths, Annabelle found that the warm air of spring had brought memory flooding back.

She suddenly began to think of Sylvester Varleigh and once her treacherous mind had started on that dangerous course, it could not seem to stop. One side of her brain cried reason and the other languished at the thought of his kisses until she felt that her mind was split in two.

She was returning to the rectory along the winding country road, only half aware of the chattering of the fledglings in the hedgerows and the large fleecy clouds scudding across the sky above. She was wearing an old blue wool dress and thought ruefully of her sisters who had pounced on her finery, squabbling and quarrelling over it like jackdaws, never once stopping to wonder if their elder sister would wish to retain any of it.

A horse rounded a distant bend of the road; on its back was a figure in a scarlet and blue uniform. Annabelle stood stock still in the middle of the road, white with terror, her heart beating fast. The clip-clop of the horse's hooves came nearer—and stopped.

"Is this the road to York?" asked a light, masculine voice.

Annabelle had closed her eyes tight with fear. She looked up.

A complete stranger stared down at her, looking curiously at the frightened girl. Annabelle babbled and stammered as she gave him the right directions. When he had ridden off, she had to sink into the hedgerow and sit down on the grassy bank until her legs had stopped trembling.

When the shock had subsided and she had risen rather shakily to her feet and walked towards the rectory, that wretched Lord Varleigh was once again in her thoughts.

What would he have thought of her home had he wished to marry her, thought Annabelle, trying to see the rectory through a stranger's eyes. All looked trim and prosperous enough from the outside, but its small dark rooms bore all the marks of straightened circumstances—the shabby furniture, the carefully darned and mended curtains, the bare scrubbed and sanded floors, and the pianoforte with a third of its tinny keys jammed with the damp. And the smell! No matter how much Annabelle decorated the dark rooms with wild flowers, there was always a prevailing smell of stewed mutton and cabbage water.

What a fright that strange soldier had given her. She wondered with a shudder what Captain Jimmy Mac-Donald was doing at that moment. Probably enjoying himself immensely, she thought bitterly. Justice had indeed fled to brutish beasts, and men like Lord Varleigh had certainly lost their reason.

THE Captain was, in fact, having a simply marvellous time. Flushed with wine and the thought of the battles to come, he was leaping through a waltz at the Duchess of Richmond's ball in Brussels.

The principal officers of the British and Allied armies were present, including the Duke of Wellington and the leader of the Netherland forces, the Prince of Orange. Several times Wellington was interrupted with messages, and the atmosphere grew tense, but the Captain was sure that battle was still far away. There was not, after all, a state of war. That upstart Napoleon had been declared an outlaw, and the combined might of the Allied forces would invade France in July and put an end to his pretensions. Meanwhile the wine flowed as if it would never stop, and the women were deuced pretty—particularly the one in his arms.

Colonel Ward-Price had married a dashing and pretty lady much younger than himself the previous year. She had saucy red-gold curls and large melting eyes and a curvaceous figure. She reminded the Captain in a vague way of Annabelle, and that and the fact that he was flirting with the Colonel's wife made him feel heady with excitement. He had several times held her much closer than the proprieties allowed, and she had dimpled up at him very prettily indeed.

The Captain felt a touch on his arm and turned with some impatience which changed into alarm when he saw the worried features of Colonel Ward-Price. He was afraid the Colonel had noticed his overwarm attentions to his wife.

But the Colonel had greater things to worry about. Napoleon had crossed the Sambre, said the Colonel. The incredible had happened. With 124,000 men Napoleon had driven a wedge between Blücher's 113,000 Prussians and Wellington's 83,000, his object being to defeat one or the other before they had time to concentrate. They must prepare to march. Jimmy was to take care of his wife and escort her to their lodgings and then join his regiment. The Colonel himself would be away most of the night.

Captain Jimmy returned to the waltz. He was intoxicated already by the wine he had drunk and was now elated at the thought of the battle being so near. And Mrs. Ward-Price was using the news as an excuse to clutch him quite closely to her delicious bosom and say with well-simulated fear that she would do *anything* to help him prepare for battle.

"Anything?" said the Captain, drawing her behind a convenient potted palm and deftly plunging a hot wet tongue between her already parted lips.

"Anything," she whispered.

AN hour later Captain Jimmy MacDonald rolled on his naked back and clasped his hands behind his head and listened to the gentle snoring of Mrs. Ward-Price who lay beside him on the Colonel's bed. It had all been very fine, but women were all sluts, really. He realised with some surprise that he didn't like them at all. Hot, messy, clinging things!

There was a soft footfall on the stairs and he stiffened and then relaxed. Mrs. Ward-Price had told him that the servants were all very loyal to her, by which he gathered she had been unfaithful to her husband before.

He was about to climb out of bed and find his clothes when the bedroom door opened and, holding an oil lamp above his head, Colonel Ward-Price stood staring into the room. His shortsighted eyes dimly made out the figure of a man in his bed. Without pausing for thought, he raised his pistol and despite his weak eyesight neatly shot Captain Jimmy MacDonald between the eyes.

Mrs. Ward-Price screamed and screamed as the Colonel, moving slowly and carefully like a very old man, carefully locked the door against intrusion by the servants.

He moved to the bed and slapped his wife across the mouth to calm her hysterics, and as she hiccupped and sobbed, he went back for the lamp and carried it over to the bed and looked down on the wreck of the face on the pillow.

"Jimmy," he said. "Jimmy MacDonald. Bedamned

to you, madame. That was one of my best officers. Could you not have picked a civilian to cuckold me with? Damn, damn all women. They never know when there's a war on."

Chapter Fifteen

MRS. QUENNELL WAS in a towering rage. She had just finished the household accounts and the results horrified her. The cost of a genteel evening "at home" in order to lure beaux for Mary and Susan had dissipated all the money that Annabelle had saved and also dug a large hole in the household budget. Carried away by the sight of her daughters in Annabelle's London finery, the usually cautious Mrs. Quennell had actually begun to believe they were richer than was the case.

Now she was faced with months of the old familiar penny-pinching. It was all Annabelle's fault. This was what came of turning a girl bookish and so she had told her husband. There was none of that nonsense about Mary and Susan—or little Lisbeth for that matter. Mary was now seventeen and Susan nearly sixteen whereas the ancient Annabelle was all of nineteen.

Annabelle had too much of her father in her. Now Mary and Susan were always happy to return from their visit to the village with delicious little pieces of gossip for their mother's ears. Lord, how they had laughed at Mary's news that Becky Blanchard's new ball gown was a hand-me-down of her sister which Mary's sharp eyes had spotted through its new refurbishing. And how Becky with all her claims to gentility—she was a schoolmaster's daughter, nothing more—had blushed *such* a red when Mary had sweetly complimented her on her *sister's* dress.

Had Annabelle joined in the fun? Not she! That uppity miss had said quietly that Mary was very cruel and had pointed out that Mary herself was wearing Annabelle's hand-me-downs and that had immediately spoiled a delicious gossip.

If Annabelle had not been so high and mighty, she could have been wed even now to the Squire's son, Tommy. But not Annabelle, thought Mrs. Quennell savagely, looking out to where her eldest daughter was weeding the kitchen garden.

She would give Annabelle extra household chores to cool her pride. It would also leave Mary and Susan with fashionable white hands.

She would have been surprised to know that Annabelle welcomed all extra work. All Annabelle craved was to fall exhausted into bed at night and sleep so heavily that no dreams of Lord Varleigh should have a chance to torment her brain.

She looked ruefully down at her hands as she paused in her weeding. They were rough and red and her nails were cut very short. An old yellow cotton dress of Mary's was hitched up round her shabby boots, and a straw hat that had seen better days shaded her head from the sun.

A familiar gray head bobbed along beside the hedge, and Annabelle drew in her breath with a sharp hiss of superstitious alarm. Mad Meg!

The gypsy woman came ambling up the path, smiling with delight at seeing Annabelle again and smelling quite frightfully. Annabelle's instinctive recoil as Meg approached did not disturb the old gypsy one bit. She was used to ladies recoiling from her and put it down to some kind of genteel attitude rather than a normal reaction to her overpowering odor.

"I don't want my hand read, Meg. Not now," pleaded Annabelle. "I'll give you something just the same."

"'T won't do, missie," said Mad Meg, shaking her filthy locks. "Meg never took money from a lady for nothing." Her old eyes suddenly looked sharply at Annabelle. "Here! What did I say last time, missie, when I was come over all funny?"

"I c-can't remember," lied Annabelle.

I really am a very weak character, thought Annabelle as Meg firmly grasped her hand and began her eye rolling and twitching act. I can't seem to be able to get people to take no for an answer.

"I see a tall, handsome military gentleman," crooned Meg. "He is going to enter your life soon. He is coming closer and closer . . ."

At that moment a smart travelling carriage came to a stop outside the entrance to the rectory gates. Annabelle cast it one terrified glance, wrenched her hand from Meg's, and fled in a flurry of yellow faded skirts over the stile at the far side of the garden and across the fields.

Meg sulkily watched her go. "Now what did I say?" she muttered. "They say old Meg's touched in her upper works but I think that there Miss Quennell's the one who's mad!

SOME ten minutes later Lord Sylvester Varleigh was feeling that he had never suffered from such an excess of gentility in his life. He was seated on a stiff upright chair in the rectory parlor and was warding off an onslaught of cress sandwiches, Bath buns, jellies, cold ham sandwiches, and fruit cake which Mrs. Quennell, Mary, Susan, and Lisbeth kept circulating in front of him while he held onto a cup of tasteless tea and wondered what on earth had happened to Annabelle.

He had already called on the rector at his church in the village and had gained that gentleman's permission to pay his addresses to Annabelle. The rector had urged him to go to the house where he would join him later. Lord Varleigh had been impressed by the rector's gentlemanly and scholarly air and had liked him immensely.

He had to admit wryly to himself that the vulgarity and pushing ways of Mrs. Quennell and her three other daughters had come as something of a shock. Mary and Susan were quite openly flirting with him, and the little one, Lisbeth, had asked him point-blank how much money he had. Not one of them appeared to grasp the fact that it was Annabelle he wanted to see, Annabelle of whom he had thought unceasingly since he had received that startling letter from Lady Emmeline.

He had realised that the Captain had been lying all along. Therefore it followed he had lied about Annabelle's teasing.

He had travelled to Brussels himself to bring about the downfall of Captain MacDonald and had arrived amid the hell and carnage which was the aftermath of Waterloo. Colonel Ward-Price had told him stiffly that Captain MacDonald had been killed in action, and Mrs. Ward-Price had burst into tears and had called her husband "cruel." It was all very strange, but Lord Varleigh had been too relieved to learn that the threat to Annabelle's life had been removed to enquire too closely into the circumstances of the Captain's death.

He wondered now as he looked from under his heavy lids at the company in the rectory parlor whether he could bear to have such in-laws as these. Then he shrugged. His home was large enough to conveniently lose them among its many rooms should they come on a visit. Then he realised with a queer little wrench that he had not yet seen Annabelle nor knew whether she would marry him.

"We have a small society here, but very select for all that, my lord," Mrs. Quennell was simpering. "Perhaps your lordship is acquainted with the Bracecourts or the Chomleys or . . ."

"Is *that* a member of your select society?" said Lord Varleigh maliciously. The elfin locks and grimy face of Mad Meg had appeared above the sill, and she was mouthing and gesticulating.

"Of *course* not," shrieked Mrs. Quennell, rising and striding to the window which she jerked open. "It is only some dirty gypsy woman. Go away. Shooooo!"

"I'm worried about missie," croaked Mad Meg. "Miss Annabelle saw the carriage and she ups and runs away. Her has gone over the fields, frightened out of her wits."

"Where?" demanded Lord Varleigh, and before Mrs. Quennell had realised what he was about to do, he had edged past her and climbed over the window sill and into the garden.

"Over there," said Meg. "Over the stile and across them fields."

Lord Varleigh tossed her a piece of gold and strode off in the direction the gypsy had indicated.

Mad Meg lovingly pocketed the gold somewhere in her rags and crept off to see if she could rob a few eggs from the hen house. It looked as if the Quennells were about to become rich and would therefore surely not notice the lack of a few eggs!

ANNABELLE lay on the grass three fields away from the rectory and stared up blindly at the great white clouds sailing across the sky. What was the Captain saying to her family? And Annabelle felt no doubt that the arriving carriage had contained the Captain, coming hard as it did on the heels of the gypsy's prophecy. Annabelle more than anyone knew how plausible the Captain could be. But it was useless to lie here like a frightened rabbit. She would do better to seek out the help of the Squire who was also the local magistrate. Now if Lord Varleigh had only been a *man* instead of a tinsel figure . . .

A shadow fell across her face, and she looked up and saw Lord Varleigh looking down at her.

Annabelle gave a shocked exclamation and jumped to her feet. "Oh, I'm so frightened, Sylvester," she cried, so thankful to see him, so overcome with emotion that she did not pause to wonder what the elegant lord was doing in the wilds of the Yorkshire moors. "The gypsy told me a military man was coming, and I was so sure it was Jimmy and . . . and . . ."

Her large eyes filled with tears and her mouth trembled as the full impact of the shock she had received finally hit her.

"Captain MacDonald is dead. He died in Brussels," said Lord Varleigh quietly.

"Ooooh!" Annabelle let out her breath in a great long sigh of relief. "I can hardly believe it. I kept dreading the day when he would come back into my life, wheedling and cajoling and being boyish and saying it was all a mistake. *You* know."

"I know *now*," said Lord Varleigh grimly. "But I was just as fooled as you. I would never have guessed had not Lady Emmeline written me a letter explaining all. When I realised that Jimmy had lied about the attempts on your life, then I realised he must have been lying about . . . well, what he said about you."

"What did he say?" asked Annabelle, trying to smooth down her shabby yellow dress.

"He said you had been teasing me and laughing at me when you let me kiss you. He said that you had a tendre for some local lad. It's not true. Is it . . . Annabelle?"

She looked up at him, suddenly shy.

A summer wind whipped across the field, rippling and turning the long green grass.

Lord Varleigh looked infinitely more handsome and more remote than she had remembered. He was dressed more for a London salon than for the country in a coat of Bath superfine, buff waistcoat, fawn breeches, glossy hessian boots with little gold tassels, and an intricately tied cravat. He was carrying a cane in one hand and a curly brimmed beaver in the other.

Annabelle looked down at her own dress and blushed. What must he think of her?

"I asked you a question, Annabelle," he said, gently watching the lift and play of the wind and the sun in the tangled curls of her red-gold hair.

"No. I-I w-wasn't teasing," stammered Annabelle, studying a crack in her boot with intense interest.

He put a long finger under her chin. "Will you marry me, Annabelle Quennell?" he asked in a quiet emotionless voice.

"Yes," whispered Annabelle, looking shyly into his eyes and waiting longingly for him to take her in his arms.

But he only gave her a very sweet smile and transferring his hat, cane, and gloves to the one hand, tucked her hand through his other arm and began to lead her gently back across the fields while Annabelle stumbled happily along beside him, dizzy with excess of emotion and pure happiness.

She then had a sudden qualm. What did she really *know* of this remote aristocrat? Just look how Jimmy had fooled her over and over again. Perhaps it was all because of Lady Emmeline's money.

She could not bear to wait any longer or to be tactful. "I asked Lady Emmeline to cut me out of her will," she said abruptly. "I trust I am no longer to receive any of her money."

Lord Varleigh looked down at the top of her head.

"I am not marrying you for your expectations, you know," he said in that old, familiar mocking voice. "In fact, you have none. Lady Emmeline's fortune is in the hands of her husband."

"Her *husband*."

"Yes," replied Lord Varleigh indifferently. "She married her footman a month ago. Any more worries?"

"None at all," said Annabelle with a happy sigh—too happy to be surprised at the news of the odd wedding. But there was *one* left. Why did he not take her in his arms?

They had come to the stile which led to the rectory garden. Lord Varleigh jumped neatly over it and held out his hand politely to help Annabelle over.

She stood at the top of the stile, looking down questioningly into his eyes, her own wide and troubled. What she saw there nearly stopped her heart.

"It's true then . . . you do love me," said Annabelle in a wondering voice.

"Of course, you silly goose," he replied with some exasperation. "Do you think I travelled all this way simply to take tea with you."

He gave her hand a little jerk and she tumbled headlong into his arms, and Lord Varleigh kissed Miss Annabelle Quennell ruthlessly, furiously, and passionately and then, pulling her down onto the soft grass under the stile, proceeded to kiss nearly every other part of her that he had always wanted to. He had meant to behave himself like a gentleman until after the wedding, he remembered vaguely, but he pushed the thought aside and gave himself up to the enjoyable pleasure of behaving very badly indeed.

"MR. Quennell! Mr. Quennell!" screamed Mrs. Quennell, staring out into the garden as if she couldn't believe her eyes. "Annabelle is behaving shockingly. I would never have believed such a thing. Oh, my vinaigrette! I have the vapors."

The rector looked out of the window, and a small impish grin played about his lips before he hurriedly turned away. He stopped his three younger daughters in their tracks as they were about to make a concerted rush to the window.

"I have just prepared my sermon for Sunday and I feel sure it would do you all good to hear it," he said. "It concerns loving thy neighbor as thyself. Pray be seated."

And seemingly oblivious to the furious glances of his wife and daughters he jerked down the window blind, lit the lamp, and commenced to read at great and boring length.

Mrs. Quennell was deeply shocked. She would never understand her husband!

Never!